Anonymous

Galloping O'Hogan, or, the Rapparee Captains

A romance of the days of Sarsfield: to which is appended the interesting

tales of the whitethorn tree, the rose of Drimnagh, and the fair maid of

Killarney

Anonymous

Galloping O'Hogan, or, the Rapparee Captains
A romance of the days of Sarsfield: to which is appended the interesting tales of the whitethorn tree, the rose of Drimnagh, and the fair maid of Killarney

ISBN/EAN: 9783337191856

Printed in Europe, USA, Canada, Australia, Japan

Cover: Foto ©Andreas Hilbeck / pixelio.de

More available books at **www.hansebooks.com**

GALLOPING O'HOGAN;

OR,

THE RAPPAREE CAPTAINS:

A ROMANCE OF THE DAYS OF SARSFIELD

TO WHICH IS APPENDED THE INTERESTING TALES OF

THE WHITETHORN TREE; THE ROSE OF DRIMNAGH; AND THE FAIR MAID OF KILLARNEY.

GLASGOW:

CAMERON, FERGUSON & COMPANY.

GALLOPING O'HOGAN;

OR,

THE RAPPAREE CAPTAINS.

CHAPTER I.

SHOWING HOW ELLIE CONNELL SENDS NEWS OF HERSELF TO HER
LOVER.—CONTAINING, ALSO, THE FIGHT BETWEEN GALLOPING
O'HOGAN AND THE CAPTAIN OF BLUE DRAGOONS IN THE SWAMP
OF MONA.

BETWEEN two of the abrupt hills which shoot out upon the Limerick plain from the wild range of Sliav Bloom, there is a deep pass communicating with level country on each side, and sending down a noisy stream to swell the waters of the Mulkern, that winds far beyond into the Shannon. To the careless or ignorant observer, this pass presents little to distinguish it from the many in its neighbourhood, save its somewhat greater depth and barrenness; but it will at once strike a person having even a slight knowledge of the art military as a spot of much importance in time of war. In the latter point of view, indeed, it seems to have been looked upon by the contending parties in the various struggles that desolated this island in former times; and well they might so regard it; for, besides leading directly to an ancient ford across the Shannon, it formed the safest outlet from the fruitful plains that lay, with all their towns and strong military positions, to the eastward.

As you proceed up the pass, about midway between its two extremities, a huge mound rises before you, with the small stream half-encircling its base. On the summit lies a heap of grass-covered ruins, surrounded by half-obliterated outworks, and a deep, dry ditch, that, with its bristling palisadoes, must have once formed a formidable barrier against the entrance of a foe. These ruins are the remains of what, about a century and a half ago, was a fortified and very strong mansion, called the House of Lisbloom.

This house, during the various wars, often changed masters; and at the period to which our story relates was in the possession of a man whom, of all others, and for very plain reasons, the surrounding peasantry least relished as its lord. His name was Gideon Grimes. The father of the worthy Gideon was an undertaker—that is, an English settler, who had made his home in that part of the country after the termination of the Cromwellian wars, and there, amidst the conquests of his bow and spear, had amused himself by occasionally hunting Rapparees, and, when successful in the chase, hanging the poor fugitives, without trial, to the next handy tree. The bold Gideon himself followed, for a time, with a high hand, in the footsteps of his departed and redoubtable sire; but with this difference, that, whereas the defunct Roundhead was consistent, and sternly held to his principle of exterminating the poor Irishry by the sword alone, the more sagacious son adopted, in the lapse of time, a safer and more peaceful method of venting his hatred upon his war-broken neighbours. Making use of the terrible laws, which, of course, were all on his side, he succeeded in driving several of the poor farmers around to beggary and death, and, seizing their holdings, thus enriched himself and gratified his inborn hatred of the unfortunate peasantry at the same time.

One instance will suffice to show the methods used by Black Gideon—for so he was called by the people,—one, too, that had an important bearing upon his after fate. It happened that his next neighbour was a farmer, named Murrogh Connell, whose ancestors had been gentlemen of large property, but who having been broken "horse and foot," as they say, during the great rebellion and the previous troubles, had left Murrogh the possessor of only a farm—a rich and large one, however—at the entrance of the pass of Lisbloom. On this farm Black Gideon had long cast his rapacious eye, concocting various plans for obtaining possession of it, all of which, in one way or another, failed. At last one of his spies came to him with the valuable information that a number of old pikes and matchlocks lay concealed in a ruinous barn belonging to poor Murrogh Connell's farmstead. This was enough. Gideon brought the law down like a sledge-hammer upon his unfortunate neighbour, ruined him, and was just on the point of turning him out of his farm, when the Williamite revolution commenced, the Battle of the Boyne was fought, and the retreating Irish armies took possession of the south of Ireland. This gave a short respite to Murrogh Connell. But the second siege of Limerick commenced; and the Williamites, in their turn, occupied all the country to the south and east. So, feeling himself once more in power, Black Gideon drove out Murrogh, who, with his herds of cattle, betook himself to the wild mountains of Sliav Bloom, and commenced the life of a kyriaght or wandering grazier of cattle.

About a week after Murrogh's flight to the mountains, his only daughter, Ellie, a beautiful young girl, walked down one evening to fetch water from a spring near their camping-place, but never returned. Search was made for her far and near, but never a trace of her could be found; and, with bleeding hearts, her father, her two brothers, and Tibbot Burke, a young gentleman to whom she was betrothed

a year previously, at length returned and told the sad tale
to her mother. Suspicion indeed fell upon Gideon Grimes,
who, it was remarked, had cast his eye upon her as well as
upon her father's lands; but nothing certain regarding him
or his proceedings could be gathered by her friends, notwithstanding that they watched him closely.

One bright autumn noon the sun glittered from the spades,
shovels, and hammers of a number of men whom Black
Gideon had employed to build up the breaches in the outworks of his mansion in the pass, in order to secure himself
from the bands of Rapparees who hung around the Williamite army, then commencing its operations upon the gallant city of Limerick. One of these labourers was a diminutive, brown-skinned, wiry-looking young fellow, who, by the
way he handled his spade, seemed no very diligent workman
in the cause of Gideon. Under a remote gable-end of the
house, he was employed clearing away some rubbish and
weeds; and, as he worked lazily under the blaze of the hot
sun, he solaced himself occasionally with a little conversation
addressed to himself, interspersed with some fragments of
ballad poetry, the fag-ends of which he ornamented with
various delectable choruses that seemed, from the way he
doubled and trebled and again dwelt upon them, to soothe
his spirit mightily under his distressing labour.

"Wisha, may the blessed fingers fall off o' me," exclaimed
he at length, as he struck his spade against some loose stones
at the base of the wall, "if I haven't found the very thing
I wanted!" He looked cautiously round him. The labourers
were all so busy at the outward wall that they could not
observe him. "Dhar Dhia!" continued he, as he bent the
tall nettles that concealed the spot aside with his spade, and
examined the spot with his black glittering eyes. "Lord
have marcy on us, if id isn't the very hole that my grand-
father entered wid his men when he killed every livin' sowl
o' the bloody Parliamenthers that held Lisbloom long ago in

the time o' Crummill! Aisy a bit, Cus Russid! P'raps the
time will come when you'll do as well as your bowld grand-
father,—rest his sowl in glory this blessed day, amin!—an'
burn the house over Black Gideon and his murtherin' villains. There's a doore for the brave Rapparees, an ids myself that'll soon take the news to them fresh and fastin'."
And with that he carefully arranged the long nettles again,
and recommenced his work and his song.

While Cus Russid—we will give him the cognomen used
by himself, which means Brown Foot—was hanging on one
of the most Elysian bars of a certain chorus, he heard his
name pronounced in a low, sweet voice from the single window above him in the gable, and on looking up beheld the
prettiest face imaginable, shaded with rich masses of yellow
hair, bent upon him with an eager and frightened gaze from
between the strong iron bars.

"Tunder alive, if id isn't Ellie Connell herself!" exclaimed he, wheeling round, and resting on his spade, "Oh,
wirra, wirra! is id here I find you?"

"Hush!" said Ellie, for it was she: "I have but a
moment. If you love my father's house, Cus Russid, away
with you, not to my father or brothers, for they can do
nothing, I fear, but to my uncle O'Hogan and Tibbot Burke,
and tell them that I am here!" and the casement was shut
instantly, and Ellie's face withdrawn.

"May the four bones wither in my brown carkiss," said
Cus Russid, "If I don't find them soon and suddint for you!"
And with that he cast his spade from him; and slinking
over, like a fox, to a half-filled gap in the outworks, he
crossed the ditch, unobserved by his companions, and soon
gained the wood that clothed the opposite side of the pass.

On reaching the summit of the ridgy hill that formed
the western flank of the pass, Cus Russid walked deliberately
to a thicket beneath a rock, and took therefrom an ashen
staff, like a pike-handle, with a small iron ring at one end,

to which was attached a piece of strong twine with a loop
at its extremity.   Again he dived his hand into the ferns,
and pulled out a thick frieze cothamore, in which he instantly
arrayed himself.   He then put his hand into an inside pocket
of the cotha, and drew forth a long, bright spear-head ; and,
after gazing upon it with great comfort for a moment, replaced it in its hiding-place, turned, and shook his fist at the
house of Lisbloom, and then, gradually sliding from a walk
into a trot, went at a formidable pace across the country to
the westward.

After travelling thus for about a dozen miles, he at
length sat down upon a height, and looked over a winding
road that led directly towards him through the woody country from the north-west.   Advancing along this road he
soon perceived a troop of Williamite cavalry, with a large
glittering cannon in their midst.   It would have been the
most natural thing in the world for Cus Russid to run away
at such a sight.   He did no such thing, however ; but, on
the contrary, using his spear-handle for a walking-staff, he
descended the height, and advanced boldly along the road
to meet them.

" What's your name, my man ? " said the commander of
the troop, as they came up.   " Come, out with it, and your
business too, for no man passes here unquestioned."

" Wisha ! " answered Cus, with a look of wonderful
sheepishness and simplicity : " they calls me Cus Russid,
sir, by raison o' these misforthunate brown feet I have upon
me.   Bud maybe your honour didn't see any cattle about
here, for my masther sint me every morthial step from the
House o' Lisbloom to look for them.   Bad luck to them, 'tis
a sore an' sorrowful journey they're givin' me ! "

" It is strange that we happen to be going to the very
place he speaks of," said the commander to the young officer
that rode beside him.   " Tell me, boy," continued he, turning to Cus, " Is it far to Lisbloom ? "

" 'Tis a sore journey, sir," answered the latter. " But maybe you're the gineral that's goin' to defind id for Misther Gideon Grimes against the Rapparees; for if you are—there! I see the cattle beyant there in the wood, an' I'll just go an' dhrive them up; and then if I don't lade you in pace an' quietness up to the very gate o' Lisbloom."

" Pass on then, and be soon back," said the captain, as he turned and followed his troop.

" Yes, pass on," muttered Cus, after meeting two dragoons who rode at a good distance behind; " but wait till I come to the rearguard, an', be the sowl of my father! I'll give you a different story to tell, you murtherin' robber."

The dragoon who formed the extreme rearguard seemed to have, from some cause or other, lagged behind. Cus Russid therefore had full time for preparation. He took out his spear-head, stuck it carefully on his ashen shaft, and there fastened it by means of a small screw. Then, like a wolf awaiting his prey, he darted down into a hollow, and there crouching amid the copse, with blazing eyes and clenched teeth, glared out upon the lonely road. The unsuspecting dragoon at length rode merrily up; but, as he passed, the deadly spear whizzed out from the bush, and struck him beneath the helmet on the neck. Almost before he reached the ground in his fall, Cus Russid had plucked the spear from his bleeding neck, with one bound was on his horse, and tearing away like a demon at a furious gallop across the country.

Finding that he was not pursued, after nearly half-a-dozen miles' mad riding, Cus Russid slackened the pace of the strong troop-horse, and rode along with a light and contented heart over the level plain, with every rood of which he seemed to be intimately acquainted. It was sunset when he gained the verge of a thick and extensive wood, that stretched along the base and up the sides of a rugged mountain. Once more putting his horse to a brisk gallop, he dashed along a tangled pathway, and at last emerged into a little sylvan valley with a beautiful stream gurgling down through its bosom. At the foot of a steep, limestone rock, that jutted out to within a few yards of the rivulet, he beheld three men sitting under a spreading oak-tree, two of whom he instantly recognised. The one nearest to him, as he rode up, was a young man of very handsome presence, tall, lithe, and brown-haired, and armed with carbine, sword, and pistol. His corselet and morion, in the latter of which was stuck a spray of green fern by way of a plume, glittered in the red beams of the sun, as he sat with a drinking-flask in his hand upon the bank over the water. The other was a man nearly forty years of age, of somewhat low stature, but herculean build of frame, and with an oval face rendered almost black by exposure to the suns of many climates. He was armed like his younger comrade, with the exception of his sword; which, from the size of its scabbard, seemed of unusual length and weight. The third, whom Cus did not recognize, was a man of far taller stature than the young man above mentioned, of a nobler and more commanding aspect, and with an eye that seemed to pierce to the very marrow of the brown-footed messenger, as the latter now sprang from his horse, and walked forward towards the tree.

"Captain," said Cus Russid, as he approached the dark-visaged man, "I have bad news for you."

O'Hogan, or Galloping O'Hogan, as he was usually called —for it was that gallant captain—started to his feet, and bent his keen, black eyes upon Cus.

"What is it?" asked he. "There seems to be nothing but bad news for us now-a-days, poor Brown Foot."

"Your niece, Ellie Connell, is in the hands of Black Gideon o' Lisbloom,—bad luck to him, seed, breed, an' gineration, I say, amen!—an' she towld me to tell you, for your life, to release her soon an' suddint."

"This is pleasant news for **you,** Tibbot Burke," said

O'Hogan to his younger companion. " But no matter. We will set Ellie free, and put Black Gideon's house in order sooner, I dare swear, than he reckons. The place this boy mentions, my lord," continued he, turning to the other,— " Lisbloom, is the house that commands the important pass I mentioned to you. We will see to it to-morrow or next day. In the meantime we had better arrange our bivouac and go to sleep after our hard day's ride; for we have much before us on the morrow. Cus, my boy, attend to your horse, which seems in a sad state—see, ours are picquetted in the wood— and then come hither ; for you must keep the first watch."

In half-an-hour after, they were asleep, Cus Russid standing sentinel beneath the tree.

The sun of the next morning found them far away from their camping-place, riding on at a brisk trot towards the east, and all laughing heartily at Cus Russid's account of his capture of the troop-horse. They were now approaching on their right the verge of a great marsh, called the Swamp of Mona, many miles in extent, and with a sluggish river ooz-ing down lazily through its centre. The track on which they rode wound along the bosky skirt of a wood, which, at some distance in advance, sent out its thickets and scat-tered trees to within about a mile of the low verge of the swamp. O'Hogan, who was somewhat in advance, suddenly reined up the stoutly-built but rather small nag he rode, and pointed to this projection of the wood. As he did so, they beheld the vanguard and advance column of an army slowly emerging into the sunlight, their arms glittering and flashing, and their banners fluttering gaily in the buxom breeze of the blithe autumn morning.

" My lord," exclaimed O'Hogan, riding back to him whom he addressed, " you see we have raised the men of Kerry in good time against the invasion of General Tettau. There he is with a vengeance ! There are his savage Danish infantry and his blue Dutch Dragoons ! "

"For a verity, I believe it is so," answered the other. "But we must be now quick to act, or we stand a good chance of having an audience of the Dutchman. My brave captain, as you claim to be general on this side of the Shannon, you must direct me what to do on the moment; for you know it would not serve the cause of the king to have me taken prisoner in an hour or so."

"Away with you, then, my lord. You and my lieutenant, Tibbot, and Brown Foot, round the marsh to the other side, and there wait till I rejoin you."

"And you," answered the other—"surely you are not thinking of one of your mad but gallant exploits this morning—surely you are not rash enough to go forward?"

"Leave that to me," answered O'Hogan, laughing. "As you yourself say, I am general here, my lord; so take my word of command for the present. Right about wheel, and fway!" And, with that, he gave the spur to his nag and dashed forward, while his companions, after watching him for a moment, galloped off in the opposite direction, so as to get round the swamp, and put themselves at a safe distance from General Tettau and his army.

Meanwhile the bold Rapparee captain tore over the moorland, not, however, directly forward, but obliquely down to the verge of the swamp; and, as he came opposite the flank of the column, halted, and coolly commenced to count the number of their cannon, and to estimate the strength of the enemy. It seemed to tickle their fancy mightily that a single man should thus put himself in such dangerous proximity to them, with a broad marsh behind him; for in a few moments, with a shout of laughter, an officer and about a dozen men dashed out from the regiment of blue dragoons, and came at a thundering pace across the moor towards O'Hogan. But they little knew the man they had to deal with. The Rapparee, after finishing his observations, turned his nag to the marsh—both horse and rider knew it well—and began to flit over it with the lightness of a plover. The pursuers at length came down, and, plashing heavily into the marsh, there soon stuck and floundered up to their saddle-girths, all except their captain, who seemed to be more accustomed to the thing, and who now led his horse warily after O'Hogan. The latter at length gained a broad, dry spot towards the centre of the swamp, and there, turning round his broad-chested nag, coolly waited the coming of his foe, who, after a few mishaps and several volleys of outlandish oaths, also gained the verge of the dry space. They were now within pistol-shot, the Dutch captain advancing cautiously on his heavy steed.

"Surrender, base hund!" shouted the latter, as he drew his long pistols from the holsters, and presented them at O'Hogan.

"Ha, ha!" answered the Rapparee: "you'll have to take me first, mynheer. Come on, then, for the honour of Vaterland, old beer-swiller, and try yourself against the four bones of an Irishman."

For answer, the bullets from the two pistols went whistling, one after the other, by O'Hogan's ear.

"Now, on the good faith of a man," exclaimed O'Hogan, "I would rather, where there are only two of us, that you had stuck to the sword alone to decide between us, like a gentleman!" And, with that, his long weapon from its sheath, and with his dark brows knit, and eyes flashing, sat prepared for the onset of the Dutchman.

"May de deevil seize thee for a damned Rapparee schelm!" roared the latter, as he thundered down upon O'Hogan, intending to ride over him, horse and man, with his heavy charger.

But O'Hogan expected this, and was prepared for it. Swerving his nag nimbly to one side, he allowed the Dutchman to rush by; and as he passed, after parrying his cut,

14   *GALLOPING O'HOGAN; OR,*

struck him on the corselet, between the shoulders, with a force that bent him forward on the flying mane of his steed. The Dutchman, however, recovered himself, and came on gallantly once more.

" I could shoot you like a dog," said O'Hogan, tapping his holster sternly with his left hand; " but no, I believe you to be a brave man after all. Come on, then, closer, closer, and let the good sword settle it between us.

In a moment the bright weapons crossed, and clashed against each other, striking sparks of fire by their deadly contact; the horses swerved round and round; again the swords clashed, till at length the long blade of the Rapparee went sheer through the side of the ill-fated Dutchman, who dropped from his charger with a heavy thud upon the boggy sward beneath. Tettau had watched the combat keenly; for, in a few moments after his officer fell, the heavy boom of a cannon tore through the clear morning air, and the shot, intended for O'Hogan, struck, instead, the poor Dutchman's charger upon the spine, and hurled it a shattered mass beside the body of its dying master.

O'Hogan, with a grim smile, shook his gory sword at the hostile army, then turned his steed, and flitted once more across the swamp, beyond the range of their cannon-shot.

CHAPTER II.

IN WHICH SARSFIELD ARRIVES NEAR THE GATE OF TIR-N-ANOGE, AND HEARS A ROMANCE FROM BROWN FOOT.—CONTAINING, ALSO, THE ADVENTURE OF THE GRAY KNIGHT'S CHAMBER.

THERE was a little book called " The History of the Irish Rogues and Rapparees," which the author happened to read in his boyhood, but on which, happily for himself, he was not left dependent for information concerning the individuals whose lives were misrepresented therein. The book had a very extensive circulation among the peasantry; and it is astonishing the number of opinions it influenced regarding the history of the times immediately following the Williamite conquest of this land, and the actions of the gallant men who fought for their homes and their religion against the psalm-twanging, snivelling, and murderous undertakers, and against the penal laws then in the flush and first swing of their gory vigour and brutality. The sorry-spirited sinner who wrote the book represents the Rapparees as a pack of ferocious bog-trotters, pickpockets, highwaymen, murderers; whereas, on the contrary, if the truth were known, they were a stout peasantry, led on by their hereditary captains, gallant and noble gentlemen, who, when dispossessed of their lands by the conqueror, took to the sword and gun as their only chance of existence, and on many a hill-side, and in the depths of many a forest and pass, poured out their life-blood trying to regain their ancient patrimonies, or, at least, endeavouring to wreak honourable vengeance upon the robbers who held them in their iron grasp. In England, the free-born Saxon thanes, who took to the woods after the Norman conquest, are celebrated in many a stirring lay, and the actions of the brave Spanish hidalgoes, who fought against the Moors, sung in innumerable melodious ballads; but the poor Irish gentlemen, who shed their blood in the Williamite wars, are only vilified and misrepresented, though they were not a whit less gallant, hardy, or chivalrous than the *Cids* of Spain or the Robin Hoods of the sister island. With this preamble, which we hope the reader will excuse, we will now resume our story.

O'Hogan, whose nag seemed to know by instinct the firm parts of the swamp, was not long in gaining the dry and rising country to the south, where, on a green knoll beneath a clump of trees, he rejoined his companions, who had thence watched with anxious hearts the issue of the combat.

"Ha! you are back at last," said the elder horseman, as O'Hogan rode up. "You had a narrow escape, captain; but, on the good faith of a soldier, it was a brave exploit, though a little hair-brained for a man of my temperament."

"You are not always in the same mood, then, my lord," answered O'Hogan, laughing; "for it was only last year I saw you perform an exploit equal in daring to a thousand of mine just now. I did it, however, to show you the manner in which Tetau will be welcomed by the bold Rapparees of Kerry. It was not my first meeting with the Dutch blue-jackets; and I hope to make them know me better before the war is over."

"I remember your first meeting with them well," remarked Tibbot Burke. "My lord, if I don't mistake, you must recollect it too. It was at the woful field of Aughrim, and on the shoulder of Kilcommodan Hill," continued he as they rode forward again. "O'Hogan and I were beyond the brow of the height, at the head of the irregular Rapparee horse, when the first troop of blue dragoons swept past us, down on the flying Irish infantry, after St. Ruth's fall. We gave them but little time to play their sabres; for we swept, in turn, down upon their rear with a clatter and a crash that they, too, will not forget."

"I also shall not forget it," said their companion, with a sad smile; "for that gallant charge aided me well in saving the remnant of our broken army."

"Who is he at all?" muttered Cus Russid to himself, as he rode close behind, listening to the conversation. "Be this blessed stick!" continued he, laying his hand upon the huge pummel of the dragoon saddle, in which he sat perched like a hawk, "but he talks as big as if he was the greatest gineral in the univarsal earth." He was not left long in doubt.

"Aye, my brave fellows," continued the subject of his

inquiries, " and I shall not soon forget the brave dash you both made at my side when we rattled down that night upon the English convoy at Ballineety."

"An' cut them into mince-mate an' smithereens, bad luck to their sowls!" interrupted Cus Russid, more loudly than he was aware of in his surprise. " Honom-an-dhial! but 'tis Sarsfield himself, an' I have been talkin' to him all the mornin' just as if he was born a commerade o' my own!"

"And cut them into mince-meat, as our little friend behind us observes," continued Sarsfield, laughing (for it was he), " and destroyed their baggage and cannon — a thing I never could have done, were it not for the sure intelligence you gave me of the enemy's movements. But what road are we taking?" rejoined he, as he cast his bright eyes over a tract of country, where, a few miles in their front, an abrupt hill towered up, with a calm lake gleaming in the sunlight at its foot. "Now that my mission in the country is accomplished, and that I have seen what you can do in the rear of the enemy, I should be crossing the Shannon once more for Limerick, where, I fear, I am sadly wanted at the present juncture."

"Your mission is not entirely over, my lord," answered O'Hogan. "You have yet to see the men of East Limerick and the Tipperary borders, and to give them encouragement by your presence for a day or two. For the rest, we shall guide you safely across the Shannon, above Limerick, not below it; which latter would not be an easy task in the present disposition of Ginkel's troops. The water you see beyond is Lough Gur, a place frequently visited by the foraging parties of the English. To the front, then, Tibbot; and you, Brown Foot, fall back farther to the rear, and keep those black eyes of yours on every bush and thicket around, for we must be careful."

In this order they soon gained the shore of Lough Gurr Riding warily round the foot of the hill that towered above

it to the north, they at length came to the eastern end of
the lake; and there, at the side of a shaggy wood, they dismounted, and sat down to regale themselves from Tibbot's
flask and the wallet of provisions he had carried all the
morning at his saddle-bow.

Having satisfied their hunger, they looked around for
Cus Russid, whose newly-awakened modesty would not permit him to sit down and join in their noonday meal; and,
after a little search, found that inquisitive individual half-
way up the hill, and peering with much apparent interest
into a hollow recess between two bowlders of rock.

"What are you looking for at the rock, Cus?" asked
Tibbot of Brown Foot, as the latter, after being recalled to
their resting-place, was in the agreeable process of finishing
his repast.

"Wisha, faith, if the truth must be towld, sir," answered
Cus, "I was just sarching for the doore through which
my uncle, Rody Condon, got into Tir-n-an-Oge. 'Tis a
quare story, an' will make you laugh, if I may make so
bowld as to tell it."

"Clear your throat first with the flask before you commence, boy," said Sarsfield, smiling. "It will enliven your
story, and mayhap enable you to add something of your
own to the thread."

"In the whole barony, there wasn't a quarer man than
my uncle Rody," rejoined Cus Russid, thus encouraged.
"He never went out in his life afther nightfall that he
didn't see a ghost,—Lord athune us an' harum!—or a
sperrit o' some kind or other. The Headless Man o'
Drumdhorn an' himself were ould acquaintances; an', as
for the Green Woman o' Tiernan's Ford an' he, they were
like brother an' sisther. The Good People—wid respect I
purnounce their name this blessed day—loved him as if
they had been his born childher; an' good raison they
ought, for he never went out on a journey high or low idout

takin' a cruiskeen o' whisky in one pocket of his cothamore, an' a dhrinkin'-horn in the other, to thrate them, the
crathures, when cowld or thirsty. Many a dhrinkin'-bout
they had together in the ould fourths an' castles by the lake,
endin' every one o' them in their promisin' to take him to
Tir-n-an-Oge—for he was morthial aiger to get a glimpse o'
the doins there—an' then puttin' him to sleep an' stalin' the
whisky—small blame to them for that, anyhow !

  " Well, at any rate, one Novimber eve, as he was comin'
home from Bruff, after sellin' four pigs of his agin the
winther, he sat down beyant there by the lake, an' drew out
his cruiskeen an' dhrinkin'-horn to relieve himself from the
cowld; for 'twas a frosty night. Afther, maybe, takin'
about twice the full o' the horn, he saw comin' acrass the
hill towards him a little ould atomy of a man, not much
higher than my knee, an' all dhressed in gray to the very
caubeen upon his head.

  " 'Wisha, much good may id do you, that same cruiskeen,
Rody !' said the little man, comin' down, an' plantin' him-
self fornint my uncle on the grass. ' Would you like to see
Tir-n-an-Oge to-night ?'

  " 'You know I would, Traneen Glas,' said my uncle (for
they seemed to be ould friends) ; ' an' many is the time, you
schamer, you dissaved me on the head o' seein' it, too. But
a cead mille failthe for all that, Traneen ! Rody Condon
isn't the man to give a frind the cowld showlder while there's
a sup in the cruiskeen. Here is health an' happiness, an' may
the wheels of our carriages rowl on pavements o' diamonds.'

  " 'The same to you, Rody,' said Traneen Glas, afther
he had emptied the dhrinkin'-horn in his turn. ''Tis a rale
sweet dhrop, anyhow. An' now let us be off to Tir-n-an-Oge.'

  " 'The devil resave the morsel of us will stir out o' this
till we empty the cruiskeen at any rate,' said my uncle ; an'
with that they tackled to, an' never stopped nor stayed till
all the whisky was gone,

" The minnit the last dhrop was swallowed, Traneen Glas clapped his hands together with a sound like tundher. Then a whirlwind came roarin' up from the lake; an', spinnin' my uncle round an' round, it drove him like a cannon-ball in through a great doore that opened bethane the rocks beyant there. It took away his breath an' eye-sight, it was so loud an' terrible; but at last it ceased, an' my uncle looked around an' found himself standin' on the verge of a great green forest, in the midst of the most beautiful counthry the sun ever shone upon. ''Tis Tir-n-an-Oge every inch of it,' said my uncle, as he went on an' on through the forest, till at last he came to a great meadow. All over this meadow were ranged thousands upon thousands of knights on horse-back, their great spears stuck in the ground beside them, their hands upon' their swoord - hilts, an' their armour glittherin'; but all seemed to be asleep, an' as still an' motionless as the ould figures upon the tombstones in Kil-mallock. At their head sat a great lord all in golden armour, with his hand also upon the dazzlin' handle of his swoord.

" ' Mille gloria ! if it isn't Garodh Earla an' his knights I'm lookin' upon !' said my uncle. The mighty earl awoke at the voice.

" ' Is the hour come, Rody Condon ?' said he in a great voice that went echoin' through the forest ; an' with that he half dhrew his swoord from the scabbard.

" ' Wisha, faith, my lord, 'tis nearly come !' answered my uncle; 'for them bloody undhertakers are spilin' an' robbin' in the world above, an' murtherin' us all like wild bastes. But wait till I come back from seein' my frinds, an' thin, if you considher it time, my sowl to glory if I don't show you the way out; for the Sassenachs want a taste of some o' them long swoords badly !'

" With that my uncle passed on—bad scran to him ! for if he answered an' said the hour was come, Garodh Earla an' all his knights would be back here in the twinklin' of an eye, an' 'tis short work they'd make o' the Sassenachs if they came. On an' on he went, till in the bottom of a green valley he came fornint a grand house; an' his heart leapt with joy when he heard the people inside rattlin' up 'Garryowen,' with a chorus that seemed to shake the very rafthers.

"'Be this stick!' said he, 'but they seem to be refresh-in' themselves inside anyhow. I'll just step in, an' p'rhaps its a cead mille failthe I'd get to Tir-n-an-Oge from some one!'

"He did so; an' the first person he saw inside was his cousin, Johnnie Harty, who, with a number of his com-merades that my uncle knew as ould friends, sat around a table o' diamond stone regaling' themselves on metheglin.

"'Wisha! a thousand welcomes to Tir-n-an-Oge, Rody,' said his cousin. 'Here, take a jorum o' this to refresh yourself, an' then p'raps you'd tell us some news from the worldt above."

"'I'll tell you one thing,' said my uncle, afther empty-ing the cup, 'this is a sweet drink sure enough, an' p'raps fit for yourselves; but, if you don't give me somethin' stronger to wet my windpipe on this blessed Novimber night, I'll die with the druth. I'd rather have one glass o' Tom Fraher's potheen than a whole gallon o' this wake thrash!

"'Well,' said his cousin, 'we can give you nothin' stronger at present, Rody; but haven't you any news?'

"'Devil a much,' said my uncle, 'an' so I'll let it alone till I hear what kind of a counthry this is to live in; for I mane to come an' settle here as soon as I can, if it shuits me, which I think it will to a T.'

"''Tis a wondherful place,' answered Johnnie. 'The first place you saw belongs to Garodh Earla, this to us, an' that beyant there to the Fenians of Erinn. Come, boys, let us show the place to my cousin, Rody Condon.'

" With that they all stood up, an' conducted Rody beyant
their own boundary into another part, where he saw all the
Fenians of Erinn encamped upon a hill; some engaged in
wrestlin' matches, an' bouts with swoords an' all that, an'
some preparing for the chase of a great stag that kept the
forest beneath.

" ' Where's Cuchullin ?' asked Rody.

" ' There he's over at the edge of the camp leanin' on his
spear,' answered his cousin; ' an' there is Curigh MacDaire
standin' beside him.   They're the best frinds now, although
in the worldt above they often had a rattlin' fight about ..1e
beautiful Blanaid, who lives now over there in that bright
palace above the stream.'

" ' Wisha! faith then,' said Rody, ' 'tis little she disarved
a palace for lavin' her lawful husband, Curigh, to fly with
Cuchullin.   If things are carried on in this way, the devil a fut
o' me will stay here for one.   Haven't ye a single dhrop o' the
crathur to wet a poor fellow's whistle afther his long journey?"

" ' Not a taste but metheglin,' they all answered.

" ' Well, that settles the question,' said Rody, givin' his
cuthamore a shake.   ' Dang the bit o' me will ever stay in
a counthry where there isn't a dhrop o' potheen to be had
for love or money.'

" The word was scarcely out of his mouth when the
whirlwind caught him up again, an' he was tossed and
tumbled, an' rowld between its roarin' wings out upon the
very spot where he had sat down some time before to refresh
himself.   He felt for his cruiskeen, but found it empty.

" ' Well,' said he, as he stood up, an' began to walk home,
' the fairies must have played a thrick on me,—bad luck to
Traneen Glas, that little imp o' perdition !   He and his
commerades drank what was in the cruiskeen, but it is a
long time till they catch me again on November night.'

" An' so that, my lord, is what happened to my uncle,"
concluded Cus Russid; " but wait till I find out the door

into Tir-n-an-Oge, an' once set my eyes on Garodh Earla an' his mighty warriors, if——"

He was not allowed to finish his sentence; for in an instant there was a rush from the trees behind them, and, before they could turn or gain their feet, poor Cus and his companions were seized by a number of men, disarmed and pinioned, and, with horse-cloths thrown over their faces, dragged through the wood, despite their struggles, and at length thrown rudely into a confined place like a cavern, where, when they succeeded in shaking the rough cloths from before their eyes, they endeavoured to look round, but found themselves in total darkness. Tibbot, who happened to be the last thrust in, put out his hand as well as he could to feel for some support, and rested it against, what seemed to him, a wall composed of huge stones placed one upon the other in the manner of those cyclopean structures, some of which are yet found in the country. Through a chink between two of these blocks of stone, a low, sharp voice now grated on his ear, like the hiss of a serpent:—

"Remember Ellie Connell, base Rapparee dog," said the voice in accents that Tibbot knew but too well, "and remember also how you crossed my path when it led to her love. Vengeance is in my hand at last; and as sure as there is a hell beneath you, you and your companions shall swing from the best branch in the wood before set of sun."

"Try it," answered Tibbott, as he wrenched the cords that bound his arms asunder. Ha! my arms are now free; and when you come for us, you will find us hard to take. Miscreant undertaker! you will pay dearly for this, if you come within reach of me, even as I now stand unarmed."

"Heed him not, Tibbot," said O'Hogan, creeping over to his lieutenant, in order to get his arms also unbound. "Gideon Grimes," he continued, as he felt his arms free, "I was often in a worse strait than this, and trust I shall live to pay you back the deep debt I owe you."

"Think of it not," answered Gideon, in a mocking voice through the chink. "Think only that you are in safe custody here; that your niece is safe under lock and key in Lisbloom; that my vengeance is in high train at last, and that you are to be hung this eventide as high as Haman, for I have sent for the ropes that are to settle all debts between us." And, with that, they heard his retreating step, as though he were issuing from an outer chamber of the structure in which they were confined.

"My lord," said O'Hogan, in a low voice, as he unbound Sarsfield's arms, "I am sorry that this mishap has befallen us, not for my own sake, but for yours. However, yonder ruffian knows you not. If he did, he would have seemed more glad of his prize. Trust to me to find some plan of escape before it comes to the worst."

"We will trust to our arms, and these small bowlders of rock beneath our feet, if it come to that," returned Sarsfield, smiling grimly in the darkness. "By my faith! an they come to take us forth, we can at least dash out some of their brains, and then make a rush for our freedom."

During all this, Cus Russid, who had slipped through his noose like an eel, had been groping about in the interior of their place of durance. Far in, in what seemed to be an inner chamber of their prison, he had discovered a round hole cut downward through a huge sandstone flag that formed the side of the roof. Through this hole, after a great deal of ingenious screwing, he had at length succeeded in protruding his black head. After looking out between the stems of the ferns that shaded the aperture, he carefully withdrew his head and returned to his companions. He had seen no pleasant sight.

"Captain," he said, as he crept up to where O'Hogan was still standing, "there is a chink in the roof inside there, just large enough for my head. I looked out through it, an' saw about twenty men undher an oak tree with Black

Gideon in their midst, an' they settlin' ropes, like hangmen, to four o' the strongest branches overhead. Oh, wirra, wirra! what'll become of us?"

"Ha!" exclaimed O'Hogan, "did you see where their horses were, Cus?"

"Yes, sir," answered Cus; "they were all grazin' in a a little hollow at the foot of a small *lios* in the wood."

"Now," rejoined O'Hogan, as if communing with himself, "I begin to recollect where we are. But we can soon settle that question," he continued, as, with a sudden start, he put his hand in his pocket, drew out a tinder-box, and struck a light. The blaze of the burning match fell dimly upon the opposite wall, and there showed the half-obliterated figure of a knight carved in the rough stone.

"By the blood of my body, my lord general!" exclaimed the brave Rapparee, the moment his eye fell upon the weird-looking and rude effigy, "but we are more fortunate than I thought. We are in the Gray Knight's Chamber, a place I know well. Black Gideon, when he thrust us in, did not know how many doors open from it, and what a treasure is hid there. Follow me, all; for there is not a moment to be lost." With that, he lit another match, and led the way into the inner chamber. Here he pulled away a tall thin flag that seemed to fit into the side wall, and discovered the entrance to another chamber. On entering the latter, they found its dry floor strewn with weapons of all kinds, from the old matchlocks and battleaxes of Queen Elizabeth's time, to the musketoons, half-pikes, and swords used in the days of the second Charles.

"Now, general," said O'Hogan, "choose your weapon. As for me, I will have this sword," and he took up a huge, rusty one that rested against the the wall. "You, too, Tibbot. You, Cus, take a short pike, and that dagger lying at your feet. You will, mayhap, want the latter in the service you are about to perform. Attend to me, boy. From this place there

are two underground passages,—one from this very chamber
that leads to the *lios*, under which you saw the horses grazing,
—see! here it is," and he removed a sheaf of pikes from the
wall, showing behind a low narrow passage,—"the other is
from the chamber outside."

"I know it, captain," interrupted Cuss. "It lades to the
other *lios*, in the very thick o' the wood. I went through it
twenty times but I didn't know this one."

"Very well," rejoined O'Hogan. "You are to escape
through that passage when Gideon and his men come in for us.
You will go through it like a weasel, while we get out through
this passage, seize three horses outside, and then ride for
our lives. Be sure to make a good noise, to draw Gideon and
his ruffians after you; and if one of them should overtake
you at the far-off turn of the passage, you know the use of
half-a-dozen inches of cold steel. Once you reach Lios na
Cummer, it will be easy for you to escape through the woods.
We are going to Glenurra Castle, where you can rejoin us."

"Never fear me, captain," exclaimed Cus Russid. "If
one o' them overtakes me afore I reach the *lios*, I'll plant this
athune his ribs. But, churp an dhoul! I hear them coming.
Give me a couple o' matches, captain. There, that'll do," and
he crept out into the second chamber, and replaced the stone
against the aperture, thus shutting out his companions from
the observation of Gideon and his myrmidons. He now
pulled away the slab that covered the main outlet, and let it
fall with a loud crash on the stony floor. At the same moment,
Gideon and most of his men came to the outer entrance, all
with brands of lighted bog-deal in their left hands,—their
pistols in the right. Everything fell out just as O'Hogan had
planned. He and Tibbot and Sarsfield gained the open air
at length, suddenly fell upon and slew the three men left
outside to guard the horses, and were in a moment galloping
away with the speed of the wind towards Glenurra Castle.
Cus Russid treaded the passage with the agility of a fox,

waited at the turn mentioned by O'Hogan, and, planting
his dagger, as he had promised, between the ribs of the
first of his pursuers that came up, gained the wood outside,
and soon put several good miles between himself and Black
Gideon.

O'Hogan intended to meet at Glenurra Castle young Hugh
O'Ryan, another and one of the bravest of his lieutenants.
But when, at sunset, they walked into the hall of that ancient
stronghold, they were welcomed to a sad scene. On a huge
oaken table, in the midst of the great hall, lay the dead body of
poor Hugh, surrounded by his weeping friends. As the three
entered, the *caoine*, or death-song, was about to commence ;
so they sat down, according to custom, upon seats provided
for them by one of the domestics, and, without a word, listened
to the wild and heart-piercing song. A beautiful young girl,
with her long black hair streaming in wild disorder over her
shoulders, stood at the head, and began the lament ; in the
distressfully plaintive burthen of which she was joined by all
the females in the room. The song went on somewhat like
the following, slowly and mournfully :—

> "The woods of Drumlory
>   Are greenest and fairest,
> And flowers in gay glory
>   Bloom there of the rarest :
> They'll deck without number
>   A red grave and narrow,
> Where he'll sleep his last slumber,
>   Young Hugh of Glenurra !
>
> The canavaun's blooming
>   Like snow on the marish,
> The autumn is coming,
>   The summer flowers perish ;
> And, though love smiles all gladness,
>   He's left me in sorrow,
> To mourn in my madness,
>   Young Hugh of Glenurra !

Sweet love filled for ever
  His kind words and glances;
Light foot there was never
  Like his in the dances,
By forest or fountain,
  In goal on the curragh,
Or chase on the mountain,
  Young Hugh of Glenurra!

When cannons did rattle,
  And trumpets brayed loudly,
In the grim van of battle
  His long plume waved proudly,
As the bolts from the bowmen,
  Or share through the furrow,
He tore through the foemen,
  Young Hugh of Glenurra!

Alas! when we parted
  That morn in the hollow,
Why stayed I faint-hearted?
  Why ne'er did I follow,
To fight by his side there,
  The red battle thorough,
And die when he died there?
  Young Hugh of Glenurra!

Ah, woe is me! woe is me!
  Love cannot wake him:
Woe is me! woe is me!
  Grief cannot make him
Quit, to embrace me,
  This red couch of sorrow,
Where soon they shall place me
  By Hugh of Glenurra!"

"It is Marion Creagh, the betrothed wife of poor Hugh,"
whispered O'Hogan, as he directed Sarsfield's attention to the
young girl who had sung the lament. "But here comes
Hugh's father, Owen O'Ryan, to welcome us. God help him!
he has a sad welcome on his war-worn face. We shall now
learn all about the death of my poor lieutenant."

CHAPTER III.

OWEN O'RYAN, the father of the young Rapparee officer who lay stark upon the table, was a man of about fourscore years of age, somewhat low of stature, with a white beard descending upon a chest of unusual prominence, and with a pair of shoulders so broad that they almost seemed to fill up the doorway through which he now issued to welcome O'Hogan and his companions. Age seemed to have little other effect upon the old gentleman than that of thinning his features, and giving a clearer outline to the long aquiline nose that projected between his sharp grey eyes ; for his figure was still as brawny and erect as when, nearly fifty years before, he had donned morion and back-and-breast as a captain of horse under the Kilkenny Confederation. He had been too much accustomed all his life long to scenes of blood and sorrow to be much affected, at least externally, even by the death of his last and youngest son ; yet as he grasped O'Hogan's hand with a silent greeting, and glanced at the woful figure upon the table, there was a tear in his eloquent eye, and a twitch upon his wrinkled face, that told the workings of the brave but troubled soul within.

"I would," he said, still keeping O'Hogan's hand in his, "that I could give you other greeting than this. But war is always the same. It has long been snapping the foundations of my house, and now it has taken my last son."

"He died the death of a brave man, however, like his brothers before him," said O'Hogan, his heart swelling and his eyes also glistening at sight of the old soldier's trouble.

" Yes," rejoined the latter, "he died at least in harness. This morning at rise of sun he rode forth at the head of the men of Coonagh, to lie in wait for a troop of cavalry who began yesterday pillaging the country, and who then carried their booty last night to the House of Lisbloom,"

"It must be the same party that our messenger told us of," said O'Hogan. "I knew they would not go to garrison Black Gideon's house without spilling some blood upon the way, and having a little pillage to keep their hands in practice. But we will settle accounts with them ere long."

"It was for that purpose my son went forth," continued the old man, "and had he only lived to meet them, they would scarcely have returned to Lisbloom. But, alas! as he crossed the Bridge of Tern, and just caught sight of the English cavalry coming out into the plain to commence their day of blood, a single carbine-shot from the wood hard-bye struck him through the heart, and there he lies." And he pointed sternly to the table. "Yes, there he lies; and there be who say that it was the man you mentioned but just now who fired the shot,—Black Gideon Grimes."

"A curse upon the hand that fired it: it was a base and coward shot," said Tibbot.

"Young man," returned the brawny patriarch of Glenurra, "curse not, for words are idle and worthless in times like this. One good sabre-cut on the crown, or slash across the breast or face, is worth ten thousand words in redressing a wrong."

"In the method you favour," said O'Hogan, "I can safely say Tibbot is not slack."

"I know it," answered the old man, "and he will soon have opportunity enough for practising it; for I have sent for my nephew, Eman na Cnuc,* whom I expect here momently with his men. Ha! Marion, he continued, his grey eyes flashing fiercely, as the young girl again commenced clasping

Edmond of the Hill.

her hands, and moaning piteously, at the head of the table, "your loss will be well avenged ere many days are over."

"We have all an account to settle with the murderous dog whose shot laid poor Hugh low," said O'Hogan; and he related the news brought by Cus Russid, and the adventure that befell them in the chamber of the Gray Knight. He then introduced Sarsfield.

The old soldier of Glenurra cast an admiring glance on the great cavalry general with whose name all Ireland was now ringing, took his hand with a clasp like that of a vice, and gave him a welcome, sad enough indeed, but still cordial, to his castle. While engaged in the conversation that followed, a slight rustle was heard in the room; and, on turning round, they beheld standing silently at the foot of the table, and gazing fixedly at the corpse, a figure that the old chief' and the two Rapparee leaders knew well, but which at once struck Sarsfield as one of the most remarkable he had ever seen.

There, erect as a spear-shaft, stood a young man, slightly above the middle height, with eyes black and piercing, like those of eagle, and a sun-embrowned face, eminently beautiful in its contour and proportions. A bright morion, in the crown-spike of which was stuck a spray of heather with its purple flowers all in bloom, defended his proud head; and from beneath it flowed down a mass of raven-black and shining hair upon a glittering steel corslet, under which, in its turn, the skirts of a light green coat fell in graceful folds over the manly leg of its wearer. Over the corselet was flung a broad green leathern belt, from which depended a heavy cavalry sabre and a long skean or dagger, with the hilt of which latter the hand of its owner was playing nervously, as he still stood gazing sorrowfully upon the pale face of the corpse. Such was Eman na Cnuc, or Edmond of the Hill, one of the noblest gentlemen, and bravest of Rapparee captains, that ever drew sword and shook bridle free in the cause of the worthless and weak-minded King James the Second.

At Eman's appearance in the hall, the *caoine*, or death-song, re-commenced wilder, more vehemently, and more distressingly sorrowful than before, the women bending over the table with clasped hands and streaming eyes; one of them, in the intervals between each portion of the heart-breaking cry, relating, in a voluble and mournful recitative in her native tongue, the virtues and various gallant actions of the dead youth, dwelling particularly on those done in companionship with his dauntless cousin, Edmond of the Hill. A number of men now filled the hall, each of whom wore a sharp iron spur upon his heel; and, whether he carried a light green cap or iron pott* upon his head, having a sprig of blossomed mountain heather waving jauntily in its crown,—a badge by which they were known through the wide country round as followers of their bold captain, Eman; just as the men who acted under the command of Galloping O'Hogan were re-cognised by their plumes of green waving fern. Several of these immediately joined in the cry; and so contagious did their grief become, that Sarsfield was glad at last to retire beyond the immediate sphere of its influence into an inner room of the castle, where, with the aged, but still warlike, Owen, with Edmond of the Hill, and the others, he sat consulting on the best and speediest method of settling accounts with Gideon Grimes and the blood-thirsty troopers who now garrisoned the redoubtable stronghold of Lisbloom.

People from all parts of the surrounding country were still crowding into and around the Castle of Glenurra, although it was nearly midnight, when Cus Russid, completely worn out, as if from a hard day's work, glided into the room in which Sarsfield and the Rapparee leaders were holding their council of war, and stood before Tibbot Burke.

"Well," said the latter, "I hope you have no worse news tell us."

"Indeed, then, sir, be me sowl! I have,—the Lord pardon

* Pott,—the helmet worn by the common cavalry men of the time.

me for swearin' before your lordship!" answered Cus, addressing the latter portion of his sentence to Sarsfield.

"What is it, my man?" asked the latter. "Methinks it cannot prove much worse than everything happening around us."

"This is it," my lord, answered Cus; "an' you, Captin O'Hogan; an' you, Edmond o' the Hill, an all o' ye consarned, ought to mind it well. When I stuck my skean into the ribs o' the first man that overtook me undher the ground by *Lios na Cummer*, an' then got out into the free air o' the wood, an' put three good glens bethune my carkiss an' the pisthol o' Gideon Grimes, says I to myself, 'Be the hole o' my coat, and be the blessed stone of Imly! Cus Russid, but you're no man, but a mane sprissaun, if you don't whip off to Lisbloom to see how matters are carryin' on there. I did so, hop at the venthure! my lord, an' found that, instead o' one throop o' dhragoons an' a cannon, that there were two throops there, and two companies of infanthry, together with Black Gideon's men, to defind the house and pass. I heerd all this from one of the workmen—a man I know, that came into the wood when I whistled for him,—be the the same token, the signil bethune him an' me was the whistle of a hawk questin.' The other throop an' the companies of infantry were sent there to furrige the counthry—bad luck to them!"

"I fear me," said Sarsfield, with a grave face, turning to the others, "that it will be now impossible for you to take this strong house, and to come at your man. Oh! if I had but one troop of my Luchan horse to aid us, we would make short work of them."

"Not altogether impossible, my lord," answered Edmond of the Hill. "Outside, in the wood, I have two hundred men, half of them foot, and well armed with pike and gun; half of them light horsemen, who will follow me to the death. My uncle of Glenurra can bring at least fifty more horse and foot at his back; and O'Hogan can have his men drawn down from the mountains by to-morrow. To-morrow, then, as sure as there are stout hearts in our bosoms, we will wreak vengeance sure and swift upon Black Gideon and his accursed house."

"Be it so," said O'Hogan, with a grim smile. "You, Tibbot, take horse and away to the mountains. Have our lads of the fern sprigs here by to-morrow ; and, by the blood of my body! if we do not cut up the Sassenach rascals, root and branch, or burn the House of Lisbloom over their heads, my name is not Galloping O'Hogan. Go on, Cus."

"You may be sure," continued Cus Russid, with a knowing wink, and a significant wave of his hand towards the western point of the compass, "afther the way I thrated the Sassenach captin over there, an' sarved the dhragoon with my pike, when I made bould to take his horse, you may be sure an' sartin that I didn't like to show my nose in Lisbloom by daylight. I waited in the wood till nightfall, an' then crep in over ditch an' bethune the pallysadoes, just for all the worldt like a weasel, for the devil resave the morsel o' me the senthries could aither see or hear, although at one time I could have tickled one o' their shins with my skean. I crep an' crep, till at last I landed myself, safe an' sound, among the weeds right undhernathe the window o' the room where Ellie Connell was confined. I wasn't long there till I heerd high words inside, an' Black Gideon spakin'.

" 'He is dead,' said he.

" 'Who ?' said Ellie, houldin' her breath, the poor crathur, as if she was on the point o' dyin'.

" 'Tibbot Burke is dead,' answered my bowld Gideon.

" 'Tibbot Burke dead!' said Ellie with a great cry; an' then I heerd nothin' but her moans for a long while.

" 'Yes,' says my cute fox again; 'an' now you are free to have a betther man.'

"The end of it was," concluded Cus, with a comprehensive glance to his auditors, "that as far forth as I could

judge, Black Gideon shook his dagger in the face o' poor
Ellie Connell, an' gave her two days to consider, an' if, at the
end o' that time, she didn't consint to let ould Habákkuk
Thrumpet-the-Word, the ould Takkum pracher he keeps in
Lisbloom—bad luck to the same Habakuk, body an' bones
an' sowl, this blessed night!—to marry them both on the
spot, if you plaise, he'd hack her poor heart into pieces not
half the size of a thrish's ancle."

"This Gideon must be as active in wickedness as the
evil demon himself," said Sarsfield.

"He is," said O'Hogan; "but his course is now run."

"Yes," said the old chief of Glenurra; "we will catch
him on the hip to-morrow. Even as I now stand on the
brink of the grave, aged and worn, I, even I, will don my
harness to have one good blow at the murdering dog, and
the rieving villains who garrison his stronghold. The last
of my sóns lies stark and stiff beneath his ruffian bullet;
but poor Hugh, at least, shall be well avenged."

Some short time after the arrival of Cus Russid, a number of women had crowded in from the neighbouring hamlets; and, as the chiefs inside listened to the important
narration of the brown messenger, the *caoine*, far more
thrilling and loud than ever, broke upon their ears at intervals from the great hall outside. Amongst these new-
comers, who, as each batch arrived, raised the death-song
in their turn over the body of the aged chieftain's son, was
one figure, far taller than any of those with whom she
entered, who now sat herself down, enveloped in a huge
grey mantle, the hood thrown over and carefully concealing
her face, in a dark corner of the hall, near the door. As
Tibbot Burke went out to get his horse, in order to execute
the command of his captain, this mysterious figure stood up,
without a word, and glided close upon his track into the
great yard or bawn, and thence out by the woodside, where
Tibbot had left his horse tied to a tree. It glided now

behind and under the black shadows of the branches. Tibbot was preparing to mount, when he was arrested by the figure, drawing the hood more closely over its features, and then, for the first time speaking.

" Ha!" it said, in a coarse, yet well-feigned voice, like that of a woman: "you are mounting, Tibbot Burke, for the, battle, just as Hugh of Glenurra mounted his steed this morning. Ere to-morrow morning is over, where shall you be ?"

"In my saddle, I suppose," answered Tibbot, quietly, " with my sword in my hand, shearing through the head-pieces of the rascals who are to come out from Lisbloom to-morrow, to rob, pillage, and slay my poor countrymen!"

" No," returned the other, " but under the gory horse-hoofs of those rascals, as you call profanely the soldiers of the brave and victorious King William. No; stark and bloody you shall lie, as he inside lies beneath the godly bullet of a true man."

"It is false," retorted Tibbot: " I tell you, I shall slay to-morrow the miscreant and coward murderer whose assassin bullet laid my comrade low. Gideon Grimes," continued he, apostrophizing one whom he thought at the moment far away, " when we meet on the morrow, take your last look at the sun; for, as sure as that sun shines, I shall slay you or die." And he ground his teeth at the thought. " Were you other than what you seem — a woman," he rejoined, turning to the figure, " I would send your head dancing over the sward with a slash of my sabre, for speaking thus."

" I am what I am," returned the figure, oracularly, and with a change of voice that made Tibbot start; " and that you will find by Tern's Bridge to-morrow: for it is there, I have heard, you mean to attack us."

" Ha, ha, black ruffian! and so we are met at last," exclaimed Tibbot, springing, skean in hand, upon Gideon;

for in that disguise the ubiquitous undertaker had come as a spy into Glenurra. In an instant the grey mantle was in the grasp of the young Rapparee lieutenant; but, with as quick an action, the undertaker slipped from its folds, raised his dagger iu the air, and struck his antagonist a blow on the chest that sent him staggering a few paces backward with the empty garment in his hand. It was well for Tibbot that he wore a good steel jack that night, else the long blade of the undertaker had dealt him a fatal blow. Recovering himself in a moment, however, he again sprang vengefully forward, but found only empty darkness. Gideon was gone; but his hissing voice sounded once more from between the ghostly trunks of the dark trees in the wood :—

"Ha, ha!" he said : "you will come to your doom, base dogs, to-morrow, at the Bridge of Tern, when we go forth to bring in forage for the army of the brave Ginkell."

Tibbot, knowing that pursuit was useless in the darkness, sprung upon his horse, and dashed away down a valley that led towards the mountains, amid the summits of which were encamped the horsemen belonging to Galloping O'Hogan.

At length the morning dawned, and the wail of the *caoiners* was hushed in the sorrowful castle of Glenurra. All were asleep in and around the castle, save those who stood sentinel outside, and those who watched over the dead in the hall. Suddenly, from the wood outside, a trumpet sent its shrill *reveillé* echoing through the silent chambers. The slumberers awoke, looked to their arms, and in an instant there was a loud hubbub and hurrying to and fro in the castle. The men hasteued out to rejoin their leaders; while the women, gathering round the corpse, clapped their hands together, and with wild shrieks raised the death-song once more, calling upon their departing relatives to wreak vengeance, sure and swift, upon the murderer of their aged chieftain's son.

Sarsfield and O'Hogan also awoke; and, choosing their arms from the plentiful collection that hung around the walls, went out, mounted their horses, and sought the wood from which the trumpet-note proceeded; and there, in a broad green glade, they found the fiery Edmond of the Hill and his veteran uncle, marshalling their men for battle. Messengers had been sent out during the night to the friends of Owen; so that the little Rapparee army was now augmented considerably, amounting to about one hundred and fifty horse, and as many foot. The latter were armed, half with long pikes, half with muskets, each having a long skean dangling at his belt; and the bright eyes of Sarsfield, scanning the ranks of the former, flashed approvingly, as he noted their brown, hardy faces and well-knit frames, while they sat their small, but burly horses, sword in hand, and in two long lines, awaiting the command of their leader.

"My lord," said Edmond of the Hill, as Sarsfield came up, "you have the best right to command here. Will you lead us for once? and I trust we shall show you, ere leaving, that the poor Rapparees can strike as hard as the men of the regular army."

"You will excuse me, young sir," returned Sarsfield courteously, "but methinks the command more befits you at the present, seeing that you are accustomed to the evolutions of those brave lads. Therefore, I will serve as a volunteer under your orders to-day, and hope, at the same time, to do my devoir like a man, with the rest."

"Well, my lord, I suppose it must be so," said Edmond of the Hill; "but, as I must thus command the whole, O'Hogan here will lead the horse, seeing that his own have not come in yet. When they do, Tibbot knows how to fall on with them like a man." To this O'Hogan assented. "My uncle here will keep by your side, my lord," continued the young Rapparee leader; "and, if he can get one good sword-slash at the crown of Gideon Grimes, why, in God's name! let him have that comfort before he dies. We must now away." His words of command rang along the line, and in a few moments the whole body was marching at a steady pace through the valley that led towards the foot of the far-off range of mountains.

After putting about a dozen miles between themselves and Glenurra, they arrived upon the verge of a bosky moorland, through which the Mulkern wound northward in many a shining sinuosity, overshadowed here and there by clumps of venerable ash-trees, that gave a peculiarly sylvan and picturesque aspect to its low, swampy shores. Out upon the other verge of this broad moorland the high peak of Comailte, the brawny giant that rears its shaggy head to the heavens in the van of the solitary range of Sliav Bloom, sent forward its rugged spurs, bedecked with many a clump of green holly or mountain ash, or shining all over with the blooms of the purple heather; and between these spurs, or hillocks, many a brawling rivulet shot down with its ever-murmuring song, and with its tiny waves glistening like silver in the golden sun of that pleasant autumn morning. From the spot on which they now halted, a broad bridle-path led through the centre of the moorland, and over a bend of the Mulkern by a two-arched bridge, so narrow that three horsemen could scarcely ride abreast over its rugged cause-way. This latter was the Bridge of Tern, beside which poor Hugh of Glenurra had fallen on the previous day, beneath the carbine of Black Gideon Grimes.

"Are the foragers from Lisbloom to cross this bridge?" asked Sarsfield, as his eye roved over and around the rude and ancient structure with a scrutinizing and keen glance.

"It is the only pass they have to the plain southward," answered Edmond of the Hill; "and we mean to wait for their coming in the wood at this side of it."

"I must certainly commend your judgment in the choice of a position," returned Sarsfield: "for the little plain between the wood and the bridge is a good spot for our horsemen to charge them when they are half over; and see, by my good faith as a soldier! at the very bridge the river takes a bend towards us, where our infantry can rake their flanks as they cross."

Again the little army moved on, and took up its position in the following manner: The horsemen, after forming in line in the wood in front of the river, dismounted, and concealed themselves under the trees, ready to mount again and charge at the word of their commander; while those of the infantry that carried muskets crouched down under shelter of the copses that clad the banks on each of the hither sides. The pikemen stood in a body under cover of the wood, on the flank of the horsemen; and thus they all awaited, with stern faces and vengeful hearts, the coming of their foe.

They had not long to wait. Before half an hour was over, they beheld the glint of weapons and armour in a winding valley that led down from the Pass of Lisbloom; and at length the main part of the garrison of that important stronghold emerged upon the far verge of the moorland, and took its way over the bridle-path that led towards the Bridge of Tern.

CHAPTER IV.

CONTAINING, ALONG WITH THE END OF THE STORY, THE BATTLE AT THE BRIDGE OF TERN; THE DEATH OF GIDEON GRIMES, AND RECOVERY OF ELLIE CONNELL; WITH THE TAKING OF THE HOUSE OF LISBLOOM BY THE RAPPAREES.

"WERE it not for my uncle, who insists upon avenging himself upon the very spot where Hugh was murdered, I would let them pass the bridge," whispered Edmond of the Hill to Sarsfield, as he saw the bright accoutrements of the enemy flashing in the sun: "I would let them pass, and then attack the House of Lisbloom in their absence."

"It would be the wisest course," answered Sarsfield; "but, now that we will soon have them face to face, we must do as best we may. And a tough morning's work we have before us," he continued, peering warily out between the trees; "for, by our Lady! they outnumber us considerably. See! our force only equals that of theirs in uniform. But look at that dark body of men in the centre, with the tall, lank horseman at its head. Who may that be?"

"It is Gideon Grimes, my lord," answered Owen of Glenurra, in a deep voice, like the growl of a crouching lion.

"It is Black Gideon himself," said Edmond of the Hill. "O'Hogan," continued he in a fierce whisper, "pass the word to have the men lie close till they get the signal to mount and charge. I will blow the charge on my whistle when the time comes." And he held out a beautifully-chased silver whistle, that hung by a small chain from a ring in his belt.

O'Hogan crept in front of the line, executed the order of the young commander, and then returned.

"Ha!" exclaimed he, on looking forward again, "here comes their vanguard clattering over the bridge at last. I hope our men under the copses yonder will not be tempted to fire at them as they pass."

"My two foster-brothers, Theige Keal and Phadrig Garv, will see to that," answered Eman na Cnuc. "They command, one above and the other below the bridge, with strict orders not to pull a trigger till they hear my whistle."

The main body of the enemy was at last somewhat more than half over the bridge, the men bandying joke and jibe at the timidity of the poor Rapparees, whom they expected to find and cut to pieces on the spot; yet whose apparent absence not a little relieved their minds, however. The half-a-dozen men of the vanguard seemed in an unusually hilarious humour; for, as they leisurely approached the wood, they chaunted at the top of their bent the chorus of a delectable and popular Williamite ballad of the day, the verses of which were intoned in a rattling, jolly, and stentorian voice by the fat Yorkshire corporal who led them :—

> "Och, be my sowl! but we've got de Talbote,
> Lillabulero bullena la!
> And our skeans we'll make good at de Englishman's throat,
> Lillabulero bullena la!"

"Yerra, then, be my sowl! if you were the father o' lies' himself, but that's thrue for you anyhow, you red-nosed robber!" muttered Cus Russid to himself from a thicket about sixty yards in front of the corporal. "Hi, hi! I could split my sides wid laughin' at the way we'll carry out yeer song, an' slit yeer windpipes, afore an hour is over."

"Ah!" sighed Sarsfield, as he too listened, "had both the subjects of that ballad, King James and Talbot, never set foot in Ireland, we would have managed our campaigns to some purpose."

"It is but too true, my lord," whispered O'Hogan in return. "Had you been allowed by the king to charge with your Lucan horse at the Boyne, that disastrous day might have ended differently."

"Yes; and all subsequent affairs as a consequence," said Sarsfield.

Still the song went on, the chorus of each verse being now taken up by many of the men filing over the bridge :—

> "Dere was an ould prophecy found in a bog,
> Lillabulero bullena la!
> Dat Ireland should be ruled by an ass and a dog;
> Lillabulero bullena la!
> And now dis ould prophecy is come to pass,
> Lillabulero bullena la!
> For Talbote's de dog and James is de "—

"Ass," he would have said; but at that moment the shrill note from the whistle of Edmond of the Hill rang over the moorland, and at the self-same instant also the half-pike of Cus Russid came whizzing from the thicket; and, as the unfortunate corporal was in the act of opening his capacious mouth to pronounce with thundering effect this last word of the verse, the weapon entered between his teeth, literally transpiercing his neck. With a horrible groan he fell from his frightened horse upon the stony bridle-way.

The first voice that broke the terrible pause that succeeded was that of Cus Russid, as he darted recklessly out from the thicket, and tore the sword from the hand of the dying corporal.

" Hi, hi, hi ! " he laughed, whirling the flashing weapon around his head—" ha, ha ! Dhar Vurrhia ! but you're a man in airnest, Cus, to dhraw the first blood on a day like this."

The next was that of Phadrig Garv, or Patrick the Rough, the foster-brother of Edmond of the Hill. Phadrig was a man of nearly seven good feet in height, and even disproportionably stout and brawny into the bargain. His tremendous voice rang over the moorland like that of a mountain bull, as he ordered his men to fire on the exposed flank of the enemy.

The third was that of Edmond of the Hill himself, as he gave the word for the horsemen to mount and charge, and the pikemen to rush out from their ambush and fall on. Then came the shouts of the English captains, as they ordered their men to deploy into line, and stand the shock of the vengeful Rapparees.

For a short time the enemy seemed to waver as they beheld the well-arranged lines of Irish horse and pikemen emerge from the wood, and heard their terrible battle-cry ringing over the sombre moor. But it was only for a moment; for, just as they commenced to turn their beards over their shoulders, as the Spanish saying goes, and look behind, Black Gideon Grimes and his compeers, with their men, came steadily forward upon their right in a well-formed line, the appearance of which had the effect of re-assuring the English troopers.   But a continuous line all along their front they get no time to form; for in an instant, with a ringing cheer that rose high over the rattle of musketry and the clash of swords, the Rapparees were upon them, with a shock like a peal of crashing thunder.   Then commenced one of those struggles, sharp, deadly, and decisive, that always ensues when the antagonists on both sides are men of strength and metal.

The English, both horse and foot, were good and steady soldiers; and their auxiliaries, the undertakers, were not a whit behind them in valour.   These men, descended from the veteran soldiers of Cromwell's armies, still nourished in their bosoms the fatalism of their Roundhead fathers; and believing that the hour of their death was predetermined from that of their birth, and, consequently, that none could die then and there unless their inexorable fate willed it; inheriting, also, a mad contempt for their Irish opponents, and a hatred of the latter amounting to frenzy, they now stood their ground, and met the gallant charge of the Rapparees with a coolness and spirit worthy of a better cause.   But, notwithstanding all this, the enemy began gradually falling back, till their whole line, with both flanks drawn in, appeared, with the gaps made here and there in it, like a torn *tête du pont* or half-moon, in front of the bridge. Round the outside of this grim semi-circle, the Rapparees, both footmen and horsemen, were now raging like so many demons.

At length the whole line suddenly gave way, and horse and foot, mingled pell-mell, endeavoured to make their escape over the bridge, the approach to which was soon strewn with their corpses; for the victorious Rapparees, with vengeful weapons and stout arms, pushed them close behind, cutting them mercilessly down as they fled.

"Blood for blood!" roared Phadrig Garv, as he rushed, sword in hand, amidst the confused throng.

"Remember Hugh of Glenurra!" shouted Edmond of the Hill, as he clove a dragoon's skull, through morion and all, to the very chin.

"Give them a touch of Limerick breach, my brave lads," exclaimed Sarsfield, rattling up the causeway, and overturning everything in his way.

"Yes, and a taste of Ballineety," laughed O'Hogan, as he slashed the bridle-hand from the arm of one of Black Gideon's comrades.

"Vengeance, vengeance for my son!" yelled old Owen of Glenurra, as he, too, went cutting right and left into the fierce *mêlée*. "Vengeance for my son! Glenurra! Glenurra, for ever! and down with the Pagan Roundhead dogs!" and the cry was caught up and echoed long and loud by his wild Rapparee followers, as they now swept their enemies, like chaff, over the gory archway of the bridge.

The English at length succeeded in getting over the bridge; and the Irish were crowding the slippery causeway in order to pursue them at the opposite side, when an unexpected messenger stopped them in their mid career. This was nothing less than a heavy iron round shot from the large brass cannon so much admired by Cus Russid a couple of days before. The enemy had concealed it as they marched across the moorland, expecting to meet the Rapparees openly at the bridge; and now, after escaping over the archway, they suddenly divided right and left, thus leaving a space through which the round shot came ricochetting along the bridle-path, and ploughing through the thick throng of the advancing Irish. The delay occasioned by this unexpected visitor gave time to the enemy to form their broken ranks once more at the other side of the bridge.

Both sides were now upon their guard; and the battle dwindled down to an occasional shot from the cannon, and a

rattle of musketry now and then from the skirmishers, who
crept out on either shore of the Mulkern. It would probably
have continued at this low ebb until night separated the
belligerents, were it not for a wild freak of Phadrig Garv,
whose warlike spirit would not allow him to remain in
inactivity so long, especially with his blood up, and the
enemy almost within reach of his long arm. Mounted on a
trooper's horse he had taken in the eginning of the fray, he
now rode over the bridge to the opposite side; and there,
reining in his steed, politely invited the best man amongst
the English troopers to come forth and meet him in single
combat :—

"For," said he, in his imperfect English, and in a
voice that could be heard distinctly at the other side of the
moor, "while our blood is hot, it is a morthial pity an' a
burnin' shame to let it cool ; an' hur own self will fight the
best *Suidhera Dheary** amongst ye for a silver skilling or a
dhuch of *Isgevaha.*"†

The stake he proposed for his tremendous game of hazard
was so low and reasonable that the simple-minded Phadrig
expected to have his proposition accepted immediately and
on the spot. A long consultation followed, however, amongst
the English, during which he several times reiterated his
cartel. At last a trooper, somewhat like Phadrig in stature,
rode forth from the ranks of the enemy, and accepted his
challenge. To it they went, stoutly and warily, encouraged
by shouts from each side—each party expecting its man
to come off conqueror. The result of it was, however,
that the gigantic Phadrig at length wheeled his horse round
and made for the bridge, with his equally gigantic antagonist
a prisoner stretched before him, beyond the bow of the
saddle, like a sack of corn taken to the market by a
Kerryman.

Seeing this, half-a-dozen English troopers spurred forward

---

* Red soldier.   † A shilling, or a drink of whisky.

to rescue their comrade, while, at the same time, about the same number of Rapparee horsemen rode over the bridge to support Phadrig Garv. Once more it came to sword and pistol between them; and, both sides being joined by the main part of their respective comrades and officers, a general and far more bloody-fight than ever commenced at the further side of the bridge. The English, who considerably outnumbered the Rapparees, succeeded in driving the latter partly back over the archway; and here, in one of those strange alternations which sometimes occur in the common course of life, but more frequently amid the shifting scenes and wild incidents of battle, Sarsfield, with Edmond of the Hill and his uncle respectively on his right hand, sat his horse at the keystone of the causeway confronting one of the English captains; while, opposite his companions, with tightened reins and swords ready on the guard, rode another Williamite officer and Gideon Grimes, the eyes of the latter glaring with a look of immortal hate into the equally fierce orbs of the warlike patriarch of Glenurra.

"I have seen your face before," said the English officer. eyeing Sarsfield keenly.

"Probably," answered the latter; "and, after this renewal of our acquaintanceship, I hope to make your memory of me more perfect. Guard yourself, sir."

The answer was a slash from the Englishman's sabre, which would have taken Sarsfield across the forehead, had he not parried it dexterously.

"By our Lady!" exclaimed Sarsfield, pushing forward in the press so as to crush the Englishman's horse tightly between his own charger and the worn parapet of the bridge, "but you give a warm welcome to an old acquaintance. However, here is to return it."

With that, after parrying another cut from his antagonist, he suddenly seized the latter by the bridle-hand, raised it, and plunged his sword deep under the armpit; then, as he was in the act of withdrawing his weapon, the tottering parapet of the ancient bridge gave way, and the dying captain and his horse were precipitated along with the falling mass of masonry, with a loud splash, into the sullen and blood-stained waters of the stream below. Sarsfield's horse stumbled over one of the displaced fragments, and would probably have followed that of the ill-fated Englishman, had not the good rider who bestrode him tightened his rein, and driven the snorting animal in a flying leap over the remaining portion of the parapet in front, and down upon the boggy shore at the other side of the stream, where we will leave him slashing and parrying right and left in the thick and raging throng of combatants, amidst which he alighted.

Meanwhile Edmond of the Hill and the other English officer were not idle. Both were accomplished and wary swordsmen ; and the fight between them would have lasted for a considerable time, had not a stray bullet struck the horse of the former in the chest. The wounded animal, probably receiving the bullet through its heart, stumbled and fell heavily forward upon its knees; and the English officer, stooping over his saddle-bow, was about to cleave the head of Edmond of the Hill, when O'Hogan, riding by at the moment, struck up his sword, and then literally sheared his head in two with one slash of the foor-foot blade he had taken that morning from Glenurra. In an instant, Edmond of the Hill was on his feet ; and, springing into the empty saddle of his late antagonist, the two Rapparee captains rattled side by side into the press in front, and left Black Gideon and old Owen O'Ryan to see it out upon the causeway.

"Ha!" exclaimed Gideon, glaring at Owen. "Remember the bloody field of Knocknanoss, old Rapparee dog, where you and your leaders were stricken by the good swords of the Lord's chosen warriors; but where you, in your profane rage, lopped off the right hand of my father. You shall now die for that sore blow, as your Rapparee son died before you yesterday by this hand."

"Yes," answered the aged soldier, "I remember that field well, base murderer, and the cuckoldy old Roundhead drummer, your father. See! this is the very sword I carried through that field of blood, and that slashed off your father's hand, so that he could never more twirl drumstick and beat the charge to call the damned Cropears into battle."

Without another word, the two enemies closed; and Black Gideon would probably have fared somewhat worse than his father at the field of Knocknanoss, had not a round shot from the cannon struck the keystone of the bridge beneath the stamping hoofs of their horses. The rickety and time-worn arch fell in at the shock; and down into the horrible chaos beneath went the two mortal foes, horses and all, the combatants around standing still for a moment at the un-wonted mishap, and then falling-to once more, more vengefully than ever. There was a struggle and then a lull beneath; but in a few moments Black Gideon bounded up the opposite bank, with his gory dagger in his hand, leaving the dead body of the brave old chieftain of Glenurra beneath the broken arch.

Although the principal English officers had fallen, others of approved skill and bravery had taken their places; and the battle would have gone sorely with the Irish, who were now all at the opposite side of the bridge, their right flank raked by the terrible brass cannon, were it not that at this opportune time Tibbot Burke came riding over the moor-land to their aid, at the head of about fifty of the fierce horsemen belonging to O'Hogan. On they came, their green plumes of fern dancing blithely in the wind, and, with a wild and vengeful war-cry, fell with sword and pistol upon the flank of the enemy. A terrible route ensued. The English infantry were now scattered and cut down; and the horse, wheeling round, swept like a scattered torrent across the moor, and away over the rough country that lay between them and the Pass of Lisbloom, the Rapparee cavalry behind them, sabring them in little groups here and there over slope and valley.

Phadrig Garv, who wished to join in the pursuit, now found himself mightily impeded by his gigantic prisoner, whom he had contrived to keep before him on the saddle through the fray. Catching the bridle of a riderless steed that stood near, he bent his large, wild eyes compassionately on his captive :—

" Hur own self," said he, " was once a prisoner, an' *e* good Sassenach released hur without eric or ransom. Sassenach," and he gave the burly form of the Englishman a tremendous shake, " take this horse and flee. It'll never be said by foe or sthranger that Phadrig Garv MocRonan failed to repay a good an' ginerous deed done to hur own four bones in the day of thrubble."

With that, he helped his foe tenderly to the ground; saw him mount and fly for his life down by the shore ; and then striking his ponderous foot upon the steaming flank of his own charger, with a relieved heart and contented mind, he set off with a hilarious roar upon the track of those that fled towards Lisbloom.

One of the English gunners who had charge of the cannon was a brave fellow, and deserved a better fate. Seeing his comrades turn and flee, he limbered up the cannon in a moment, leaped upon the leading horse of the team that drew it, applied his whip, and was in the act of galloping away, when Cus Russid, who was gliding like a little demon everywhere over the field, presented a pistol, and shot him through the head. And thus Cus took upon himself the credit of capturing the cannon he so much admired.

It was now about half an hour after the commencement of the pursuit, and Cus Russid and several of his companions

were congregated around the gun, debating amongst themselves how to dispose of it, when a horseman came spurring
back with an order from Edmond of the Hill to take it
forward to Lisbloom, in order, if necessary, to batter down
the defences of that stronghold. The triumphant Cus seated
himself in a moment astride upon the breech of the gun,
while some of his comrades mounted the horses; and away
they went, attended by a jubilant crowd of pikemen. Now,
Cus Russid, as the reader was made aware on his first
introduction to that lively individual, had a particular *pen-
chant* for singing songs on every possible occasion. Deeming
the present a more than usually favourable one for indulging
his musical propensity, after kicking up his heels in the
excess of his delight, and calling for attention from his noisy
comrades, he rattled forth in an exceedingly lively and merry
strain,—

" THE PRODESTAN' GUN.

" There are threasures in Ireland as good as a throne,
  Mighty pleasant an' fine, could we make them our own;
  An' this Prodestan' gun is a very fine thing
  Fwhen it fights for ould Ireland and Shemus the king.
  Yet to-day in the fray, be my sowl! 'twas no joke,
  Fwhen its Prodestan' balls through the Rapparees broke;
  But its race 'nathe the sway o' the Dutchman is run,
  For the Rapparees now own this Prodestan' gun!

Chorus, boys! Fwhilst there's life there's hope, as the worm
said in the stomach of the gamecock.

Dum erlium di tay, dum erlium ri da,
Dum erlium, fol edrium, dum murlium ri da!

Whist! 'Tis time to stop yer windpipes, ye divvels. Here
goes again, as the snowball said when it hit Nancy Doornan
on the nose.

'Tis nate at the patthern to dance a moneen;
'Tis nate for to sit by a purty colleen;
'Tis sweet for to bask by a hedge at your aise,
Fwhen the winds are all warm an' the sun in a blaze;

There's a plisure in striking your innimy sore;
There's a plisure in friendship an' whisky galore;
But the greatest o' plisures that's ondher the sun
Is to turn to a Papish this Prodestan' gun!—

Chorus! chorus! chorus! as the wran said afore he cracked
his windpipe.

Dum erlium di tay, dum erlium ri da,
Dum erlium, fol edrium, dum murlium ri da!"

A burst of laughter hailed the termination of Cus
Russid's song; at which that facetious personage kicked up
his heels upon the cannon again, and seemed mightily pleased.
When they at length arrived at a turn in the pass that
brought them in view of the stronghold of Lisbloom, a sight
presented itself before them that at once arrested their further
progress. To explain it, it is necessary to go back half an
hour or so.

When Black Gideon—who, with a dozen of his comrade
undertakers and about thirty troopers, seemed to fly on the
wings of the wind—reached his house and took shelter
behind its fortifications, the Rapparees, headed by their
leaders, were just entering the open gorge of the pass.
Gideon, seeing that the place was no longer tenable against
the victorious force of the Rapparees, told all whom he met,
and those that entered with him, to shift for themselves,
and then rushed up a winding stair that led to the room in
which Ellie Connell was confined. Bearing the fainting
girl in his arms down the stairs and out into the bawn, he
took a fresh horse, placed Ellie before him on the saddle,
and, dashing out with the rest through the open gate, followed their course up the pass for a few moments, then
turned aside, and swept obliquely across the breast of the
hill, in order to gain the shortest track leading to Ginkell's
camp before Limerick.

It was therefore that Cus Russid and his companions, as
they halted, beheld the Rapparees pursuing the pani-

stricken remnant of the garrison up towards the high outlet of the pass, and two horsemen riding, one in pursuit of the other, across the declivity of the hill. Cus recognized them in a moment.

"Be the sowl o' my father!" he exclaimed, "if it isn't Black Gideon himself, with Ellie Connell afore him on the saddle! An' see, there is Tibbot Burke hot fut upon his thrack! That's it Tibbot!" he shouted. "Don't spare the spur till you come at him with the good swoord or pisthol. Hurry, hurry, hurry! for you have a fast rider and a desperate man to dale wid. Och! they'll be soon out of our sighth round the showldher o' the hill."

"No," said one of his comrades; "Tibbot is gettin' above him, an' will make him turn down into the glin o' Darren, fwhere we can see it all out bethune them. Dhar, Dhia! bud it'll be grand,"

"Divvel a bit!" returned Cus: "he's too cute for that, boys. Look, look! he's goin' to ride down the side o' the Coum Dearg," alluding to a deep scaur or glen that ran down the side of the hill; "an', if he gets into it, the sheep-thrack will take him out over the summit, bad luck to him on his journey! Hurry, Tibbot, hurry! He's facin' it, an see how the hoofs of his horse sthrike fire from the flinty stones! Hurry, Hurry, Tibbot! or Black Gideon will give you the slip. Ha! honom-an-dhiall, he's down!"

It was just as Cus Russid said. Gideon's horse struck one of its fore hoofs against a stone, stumbled, and then fell forward; Ellie Connell, luckily for herself, dropping quietly off upon the grass at the upper side; and Gideon, with a vain effort to recover himself, at length rolling over and over for a space down the hill. He was on his feet in an instant however, and, drawing two pistols from his belt, stood prepared for Tibbot who was now approaching at full speed. As the latter drew near, Gideon suddenly turned, with a diabolical and sinister leer upon his face, and discharged one of the

pistols at Ellie, as she still lay senseless upon the grassy slope.
The ball ploughed up the earth within half a foot of her head,
but did no harm.   The other pistol he got no time to use;
for, as he wheeled round to take aim at his coming foe, the
sword of Tibbot descended upon upon his neck, half severing
the head from the quivering trunk.   Thus fell Black Gideon
Grimes ; and the last mortal sound that rang in his ears was
an exultant yell from the gorge beneath of the poor peasants
whom he had oppressed and plundered of the little left them
by war and tyranny in their native glens.

Ellie Connell soon recovered from her swoon ; and, by
the time she was conducted to the bottom of the pass beneath,
most of those engaged in the pursuit had returned.   There
Tibbot presented his future bride to Sarsfield, who, wi ⁓ a
pleasant face, wished them many a happy day togethe ;—a
wish that was afterwards fulfilled.   Sarsfield then bade , hem
farewell ; and, with a mighty cheer that woke the ech ᴊ₃₃ of
the surrounding hills ringing after him, rode up the pass,
accompanied by O'Hogan and his horsemen, who were to
conduct him across the Shannon to Limerick, leaving Edmond
of the Hill and his victorious Rapparees to occupy the doughty
stronghold of Lisbloom for the service of King James the
Second.

THE WHITETHORN TREE.

A LEGEND OF KILCOLMAN CASTLE

CHAPTER I.

They washed the blood, with many a tear,
   From dint of dart and arrow,
And buried him near the waters clear
   Of the brook of Alpuxarra.

SPANISH BALLAD.

THE principal boundary between the counties of Cork and Limerick is that abrupt and boggy range called by Spenser the Mountains of Mole, but in the Irish denominated Sliabh Ballyhoura, or the mountains of the dangerous ballaghs or passes. To the west and south of this range, over many a broad plain and undulating valley, once spread the wild and romantic Forest of Kilmore. In the days of Elizabeth, and for nearly a century after, this forest sent out many off-shoots into the neighbouring baronies. One of the most considerable of these branches, commencing near Buttevant, swept round the southern declivity of the Ballyhouras, until at length it formed a junction with the great and intricate woody fastness of Aherlow, at the base of the Gaulty Mountains. Through it ran the beautiful Mulla,—now called Aubeg,—a short distance from which, on the shore of Lough Ullair, or the Eagle's Lake, rose up the battlements of Kilcolman Castle, once the residence of the immortal Spenser. This castle anciently belonged to the Earl of Desmond; but in July, 1586, it was granted by the crown to Spenser, together with about three thousand acres of the surrounding country. Here Spenser wrote his "Faërie Queen;" here—

> He sat, as was his trade,
> Under the foot of Mole, that mountain hoar,
> Keeping his sheep beneath the cooly shade
> Of the green alders by the Mulla's shore,—

when the "Shepherd of the Ocean," Sir Walter Raleigh, visited him; and here he remained until the October of 1598, when the Desmond Insurrection broke out, and the castle was taken and burnt by the exasperated Irish. An infant son of his was burnt to death in the flames; and Spenser himself, together with his wife and two other sons, narrowly escaped sharing the same fate, and fled to England, where, on the 16th of January, 1599, he died at Westminster, London. The castle is now a mere ruin; but, from the distance at which it can be seen, and its charming situation on a green knoll above the lake, it still forms a very picturesque and interesting feature in the landscape.

It was a calm autumn evening, during the great insurrection which commenced in the year 1641. The waterfowl were quietly swimming on Lough Ullair; and the rich sunbeams were bathing the castle in their mellow light, and showing distinctly out the black, stern traces of the fire which loosened and disfigured its walls nearly half a century before. Outside the castle all was brightness, life, and beauty; but inside, darkness and decay made their dwelling throughout all the deserted chambers, except one, whose gloom was dispelled by a merry little charcoal fire, which burned like a luminous point on the huge fireplace. Two figures sat on a stone bench beside that fire: one, a tall, dark-complexioned woman, advanced in years; the other, a young and handsome girl. The countenance of the latter showed the traces of recent weeping, b　seemed beautiful even in its sorrow; and its effect was brightened by the tresses of rich, amber-coloured hair which fell in bright masses upon her shoulders, harmonizing sweetly with the graceful folds of her dress, as she sat turned towards her companion, who was in the act of addressing her.

"You'll not have him, you say. You'll never more meet a truer or braver man. If you saw him, as I did, in battle, when he was surrounded near Glanore, an' how gallantly he broke through that press o' men, you'd change your mind soon an suddint."

"I cannot change my mind," answered the young girl: my mind an' heart are made up, an' true to another since I was a child; an' death itself cannot make me break the faith I plighted."

"Well, I know him too. But you see by this that you can never be his wife, for you'll never see his face more. Take the man that suffered for you, an' that got himself hunted, like a wild baste, through the mountains for your sake. If you don't, you'll have his etarnil revenge on you, an' mine too,—an' you know me well by this; an' you must choose between bein' his wife, an' going into the arms o' the Black Captain."

"The Black Captain cannot be worse than your black brother. I'll meet the fate that God wills me, an' still be true to the man I love. Death will soon end my misery, if it comes to the worst."

At this moment a step was heard descending the spiral stair that led to the apartment above. The old creaking door opened, and the Black Captain himself stood before them. He was a man past the meridian of life, of an exceedingly dark complexion, and wearing the high hat, sober-coloured cloak, and large, plain, iron-hilted sword of a Puritan.

"Hast thou told her," he said, addressing the elder female, "of the blissful life she is to lead with a warrior from among

God's chosen ? Methinks thou must have a most persuasive
tongue; for Reuben Sadface, my trusty man, knows by this
the sore persuasion that dwells in thy clenched hands and
finger-nails."

"I've towld her all," answered the woman, sullenly, "an'
she's the same still. Ask herself."

"I may not beautify my soul with such loving dalliance
this eventide. A blessed and holy call, a war call, has taken
possession of my spirit for the moment. Even as Saul was
commanded to slay the idolatrous nations, so am I chosen to
purge by the agency of fire and steel the western valleys of
their heathenish progeny; and I must be gone. When the
sword of the Lord shall have fallen upon those children of
Baal, I shall return to tell what I have left unsaid to this,—
this branch rescued from the burning,—this most fortunate
of maidens."

"Alice O'Brien," said the woman bitterly, when the
Black Captain had left them, "answer me this. Do you
think I coaxed you up an' thrated you like as if you wor my
own sisther, to be bate and baffled by you this way?   Maybe
you won't be the show for all Murrough an' Theothawn's *
army, when the Black Captain has you in his crooks! Maybe
then you'll wish to be back with me, and that you had made
up your mind to have my brave brother Theige, my fine and
cunnin' damsel !"

"I answer once more," said Alice, "that I'll have neither
the Black Captain nor your brother Theige: I'll die first.
I put my trust in God; an' perhaps my brother Moran an'
his comrade, John MacSheehy, may come soon enough with
their horsemen, an' set me free."

"Your brother Moran an' your sweetheart John have
enough to do to keep their own carkisses safe, without mindin'
what'll become o' the likes o' you. But never mind. Wait,
an' we'll see what'll come o' this to-morrow."

* Murrogh the Burner.—the Earl of Inchiquin.

A few hours after the departure of the Black Captain that evening, the setting sun was darting his red beams through the glades of the scattered forest by the banks of the beautiful Ounanar, a few miles eastward of Kilcolman Castle. The Ounanar is a wild stream, rising far up in the Ballyhoura Mountains, amid the bogs beyond Kilcolman, and flowing into the Mulla a short distance below Doneraile. In one of the most solitary glades beside the stream, the sunbeams were reflected by some not very unfrequent objects in those dreadful times, namely, the morion and accoutrements of a dead young soldier. He lay upon his back, with his right hand grasping the empty scabbard of his sword, and his left thrown upward threateningly, as if, in his last moments, he had endeavoured to menace death or some other unwelcome visitor from his side. His head, cleft by a great wound, lay heavily upon the blood-stained grass; and his morion, also cleft, had fallen off, part hidden in the grass, and the top, or spike, glittering in the sun. As he lay thus, a raven from a neighbouring tree perched upon a fragment of rock near him, and for a few moments regarded him with a wary and inquisitive look; then, as if satisfied that there was no danger, it half-opened its wings, and, hopping along the grass, alighted again upon the spike of the morion. It was, however, soon scared from its unsteady resting-place by a more rapacious banqueter. A huge wolf rushed forth from the copse, and, with a voracious whine, laid its foremost paws upon the iron-clad but pulseless breast of the young man. Its long white teeth ground against the edge of his steel breastplate, its red eyes glared with ferocious satisfaction at the prospect of its savage meal, when it was in its turn also interrupted, but in a more fatal manner. A shot rang up from the river bank; and the wolf, wounded through the heart, fell backward, with claws and teeth tearing in its mortal agony a huge frieze cloak or cape, which lay over the shoulders of the dead soldier. Before the echoes of the shot had died along the hollow banks of the stream, a horseman rode swiftly up the glade, and, leaping from his steed, plunged his sword through the body of the expiring wolf.

The horseman was attired like the young soldier, whose body he had thus opportunely rescued. On his head he wore a helmet, or morion, without a plume, but with a sharp steel spike projecting straight upwards from its crown. Over his shoulders, and reaching beyond his hips, hung a brown frieze cape, fastened at the throat by a silver clasp, and open somewhat in front, showing underneath a bright steel back-and-breast, or corselet. His trousers were coloured like the cape, and of the same material, the legs falling below into a pair of long unpolished boots which reached to his knees, with their formidable spurs, giving him the air of one by whom the saddle was very seldom abandoned for a more quiet seat. From a belt around his waist, along with the usual skean or dagger, hung the scabbard of his sword; and in his right hand he grasped the naked blade, while in his left he held the small musketoon which he had just discharged with so true an aim. He was young, somewhat about the middle height, and his bronzed, determined face and fearless eye showed that he had seen both hardships and dangers, and was ready to brave them again without concern.

He advanced now, and stooped down, examining the features of the fallen youth. " Ha, Moran !" he exclaimed, suddenly, "great God, how is this?" Then falling on his knees beside the body, he continued, " O Moran! my only friend, and the brother of my lost Alice, little I expected we'd meet thus! Little did I think that 'twas your dead body I was saving from the jaws of the wild dog of the hills! The battles are coming again, and the gallant gathering is by the walls of Castle na Doon ; but who will ride beside me like Moran O'Brien ?"

He started to his feet as if the thought maddened him, and commenced striding wildly up and down the glade.

" Poor Ellen Roche, too, who loved him so well!—little

ner light heart dreams of this,—the black and woful news
I'll have to tell her at the dance to-morrow!

He once more approched the body, and, examining it
more minutely, found a bullet-wound in the throat, which,
with the severed helmet and the long gash upon the head,
made him suspect that the unfortunate young soldier had
come by his death unfairly. Then, as if his suspicions
had lighted upon some individual, and that he determined
to wreak immediate vengeance, he took the body in his arms,
and deposited it in a deep, narrow rent between two rocks
near the stream; and covering it with some leafy boughs, and
a few long stone flags, in order to preserve it from the wolves,
at that period so numerous in the country, he muttered sorrowfully a few prayers, mounted his steed, and departed.

After crossing the river, and riding along its eastern
shore somewhat more than a mile, he turned his horse's head
towards the southern flank of a steep mountain, strewn with
great boulders of rock, which, as the twilight now darkened
over the hills to help the illusion, rose up from the solitary
heath, bare and spectral, like the deserted and melancholy
ruins of an ancient city. A number of these lay congregated in an irregular ridge near the summit; and here the
young horseman alighted, and, leading his steed noiselessly
along the soft turf, stood at length beside a huge, broad rock,
so flat and low that it scarcely reached above the brushwood
and long heath that grew around. Underneath it, at one
side, there was a small entrance, or opening, through which
a confused jumble of voices now fell upon the horseman's
ear; while a clear stream of light also shot forth, and
brightened the scarred and weather-beaten face of a crag that
rose hard by. Peering cautiously through another and a
smaller chink, he beheld, what he indeed sought for, a group
inside; the individuals of which corresponded exactly in
appearance with the strange place they had chosen for their
habitation.

In the corner of a small apartment irregularly formed by a rent in the crag, and having for its roof the lower surface of the flat rock mentioned above, sat before a bright fire of blazing bog-deal three figures, as different in appearance from each other as could be consistent with the fact that each formed a member of the great human family. He who sat between the other two was a man in the prime of life and of gigantic stature; his long matted beard and hair falling almost on his breast and shoulders, and a reddish cap, with a sprig of blossomed whitethorn for a plume, set somewhat cavalierly, but fiercely, on his head. His prominent, beard-covered chin, and thin, beaked nose, gave to his wild physiognomy a sinister expression, which was increased by a pair of gloomy eyes bent sternly on the person at his right, whom he was in the act of addressing. He was enveloped in a soiled scarlet cloak, which lay closely around his upright figure, and fell in folds behind him upon the block of stone on which he sat, showing a pair of long, frieze-clad legs, and feet encased in great brogues, with low heels, made so in order not to impede his progress over the quagmires and bogs of which he was so often a denizen. Such was the figure of Theige Folling Dearg, or Timothy of the Red Cloak—the dweller by the Fairy Thorn-Tree of Glananar. He to the right, to whom Thiege of the Red Cloak gave in his conversation the title of Thiege Cu Allee, or Thiege the Wolf, had full and ample claims, in appearance at least, to that sylvan cognomen. He was of dwarfish height, but, at the same time, so brawny and broad-shouldered as to have, as he sat with his short legs stretched out and hidden among some green heath, the appearance of a giant ogre, sunk to his middle in the earth. His mouth, the most prominent part of his features, was garnished with an irregular set of large teeth, which gave him, when he either laughed or sneered, some resemblance to a snarling wolf. He wore a cap and loose frieze coat, open in front, and showing a broad

hairy chest, not unused, if one could judge from the wild
expression of the face, to heave with many a storm of vindictive passion. Their comrade was, in form certainly, a
direct opposite to both. His features were regular and
handsome; he appeared, as he sat, a little below the middle
size, and very slenderly formed; but their was a wiriness
about his whole frame, and something in his dark, sagacious
eye, that told him no mean antagonist, with that long skean
he wore at his side, in a single encounter or in the confusion
of a battle. His clothes fitted better than Cu Allee's, but
were of the same material. He answered his companions
with the utmost self-complacency, when they addressed him
in their discourse by the enviable title of Theige na Meerval,
or Timothy of the Wonders,—a name to which he had, at
the moment, strong claims, from the miraculous facility with
which he disposed of some large fragments of beef he had
boiled upon the bog-deal embers. Various instruments of
warfare were strewn around them, demonstrating, that, in all
circumstances, excepting that of a blockade, the citadel could
be held for a long time, and against considerable odds. They
appeared to be engaged in some very interesting conversation.

"For hurself," said he of the Red Cloak, " hur would
rather see the Sassenachs with their spurs in their horses'
flanks, an' their soords in their hands, nor to see them slinking
behind stone garrisons, like foxes in the crags of Ullair."

"Yes," said Cu Allee, in his native tongue, "wherever
the Sassenach goes, there is rich booty ; and, for me, there
was once sweeter booty—plenty of revenge."

"Hur often heerd Cu Allee whisperin' and cugkerin', in
hur sleep and in hur wake, about that revenge, but never
heerd how 'twas got."

" 'Twas got," said the Man of Wonders, pointing to a
suspicious-looking bundle of twisted osiers by the side of Cu
Allee, " 'twas got, I'm sartin, in the ould way, by the gad
an' cross-sticks."

"'Twas got," exclaimed Cu Allee fiercely, "on the day that Murrogh and Theothwan's captain, with his guard about him, gave into my hands Rory Finn, the black and cursed ruiner of my young sister. The clink of the Sassenach's gold was sweet; but far sweeter was Rory's groan to my ears, when he knew his time was come. We placed the cross-sticks beneath the walls of Kilcolman; and I—I faced Black Rory towards the darkened home and the churchyard where she slept near, and sent him, for good or for bad, to follow her to his last account. Many is the gad I twisted about the neck of Gael and Sassenach; but the one that finished my mortal foe, Rory Finn,—and I have it here beside me,—was the most precious of all."

"Hurself woud take it by the strong hand an' the sharp soord, as hur did last night," rejoined Folling Dearg.

"Or," said the Man of Wonders, holding out his long, bright skean in his hand, "or by manes o' this, as a sartin persón did not long ago in Kilkenny. Listen; for it is one o' the charmin' things that brought me into the sarvice o' the prayer-canters,—the bloody, timber-faced Parliaminthers. I was standin' in a sthreet in Kilkenny, before the doore of a big forge, where the smiths, from home an' from furrin parts, wor hammerin' an' sledgin' away at soords an' pikes an' armour an' skeans, the dead brother o' this I hould in my hand. I was standin', doin' a few tricks o' sleight-o'-hand, an givin' a few summersets in the way o' my business; an' the smiths, with their black faces an' brawny arms, wor beginnin' to throw away their hammers an' sledges, an' come to the doores an' windows, lookin' at me, when who should come along at the other side o' the street but a grand bishop, or cardinal, with five or six big fellows, like sogers, walkin', some behind him an' some before, with drawn soords in their hands. He looks at the smiths all idle, an' the arms wantin' so much for the war; an' he looks at me playin' my capers in the street. He said somethin' to the men in a furrin lan-

guage; an' three o' them made over to me, an' laid hoult o'
me worse than if I was caught in a big vise in one o' the
forges, an' then banged me and bate me with their sword handles
off o' the street. I said nothin', but followed them for a
while, till the man that laid hoult on me first was sent on a
message beyond one o' the gates o' the town-wall. I waited
in the porch for the bloody villain; an', when he was comin'
past me, I gave this sportin' skean o' mine a nate night's
lodgin' in his side, an' fled for my life, an' won the race like
a man."

One part of this most edifying conversation, namely,
Folling Dearg's allusion to his deed of the preceding night,
interested the listener outside not a little, wanting, as he did,
to find some clue to the death of his comrade; but it seemed,
on the present occasion, he had business of even more importance to himself to transact with these worthies; so,
making a slight noise as a signal of his approach, he walked
round to the large aperture in order to enter. Na Meerval,
when they heard the sound inside, crept out with the agility
of a weasel, through the small chink; so, when the young
horseman entered, he was somewhat surprised at finding only
two inside.

"I thought," said he to Folling Dearg, the moment he
had entered, "that Na Meerval sat by your side now."

"Na Meerval stands by your side," answered Folling
Dearg, eyeing the visitor darkly.

That lively personage, having entered at the large aperture as stealthily as he before had made his exit, stood close
at the side of the horseman.

"Theige Na Meerval is here," said he. "When he
found the fern-seed by the Robber's Well, the Shee Geeha
became his comrade; for he could make himself be seen or
not be seen, whenever he took it into his head. Shane na
Shrad knew this before, I think."

Shane na Shrad, or John of the Bridle—a name, by the

way, which the young soldier had got in consequence of his feats of horsemanship—was too sharp-witted to be deceived so readily.

"Shane na Shrad knows," he said, "that there is a chink, besides the door, in this cavern.'

"Fwhat does hur come for now?" queried Folling Dearg, who, although he pretty well knew the purport of the visit, wanted to obtain some information from John of the Bridle. "To-morrow is hur great day by the walls of Caishlern na Doon; but Theige Folling Dearg knows that, like a flock of wild duck from the springs, the Gael will be scattered soon by Murrogh of the Burnings and his brave Sassenachs."

"Murrogh and his starved wolves are not likely to do so at present," said John of the Bridle. "You, I know, and your two comrades, are on the scent for news, to be paid for it by the gold of Black Murrogh of Inchiquin. We keep it no secret that before long we'll be passing the Bridge of Donneraile; and you and its defenders may dream of what's to follow, while our troopers are dancing with the girls for a day or two beside the green woods of Castle na Doon."

"In my mind," said Na Meerval, "some of them will caper a quarer dance in a short time, undher a kind of three, where they've have only the wind for a floor, an' Cu Allee's thrue-lover's knot about their necks."

Cu Allee, although he principally exercised his genius in the enviable profession of a skibbioch, or hangman, never relished a jibe, however, on that score.

"Cu Allee's knot," he exclaimed, "was once round your neck; and, only he let you practise your sleight-of-hand upon it, you'd dance the skibbioch's jig. But the next time——"

"No more of this," said John of the Bridle. "I came," he continued, addressing Folling Dearg, "that you may now redeem the promise you gave me when we last met among the mountains. Where is Alice O'Brien?"

Folling Dearg's face darkened as he spoke. "Hur has searched hill-side an' coom an' town an' forest since for a colleen with a thrue heart, like the one you towld hur of, but never found one since. Maybe the Black Sassenach captain could tell all about hur."

"Is this, then," said the horseman, "the way you pay me for giving you your life when the troopers were about cutting you in pieces, and Moran O'Brien standing with his skean at your throat?"

Folling Dearg laid his hand on his skean, as if to guard against the consequence of what he was about to say. "Iss, maybe Moran O'Brien knows by this what it is to put a skean to a brave man's throat, an' threaten him with death. An' Alice, hur is false to Shane na Shrad as well as to—to Folling Dearg; an'," he continued, with a deadly and vindictive sneer upon his lip, "hur can now smile upon the Black Captain in the camp-tents o' Murrogh the Burner."

"Lying villain," exclaimed the horseman, "here is pay-ment for your treachery." And, suddenly drawing out his sword, he struck Folling Dearg with its pummel upon the forehead. Folling Dearg reeled, and fell among the heath in the corner of the cavern. But, recovering in a moment, he sprang to his feet, with the fury and agility of a panther, and, seizing a long sword that lay against the wall beside him, struck at the horseman a blow that would have gone, spite of guard and helmet, to his brain, had not the blade, as it swang upwards, come against the low roof of the cave, and shivered into a hundred fragments. At this moment, and while both were preparing to dash again at each other, the two hopeful spectators of the encounter rushed between them.

"We'll have no more fightin' to-night," said the Man of Wonders: "Shane na Shrad saved Cu Allee's life, an', afther that, Cu Allee saved my life; so 'tis Shane I must thank that all the ravens in the country haven't me in their hungry craws at present. So, we'll stand to Shane na Shrad this time, an' have no bloodshed to-night in our nate an' paceful little castle."

"Stand to hur, then," said Folling Dearg; and, with that, he sprung, skean in hand, at the horseman. But he missed his aim; for, at the same moment, Cu Allee threw his long arms around his knees, and dragged him by main force to the other corner of the cave, where, with his face streaming blood, he stood struggling and glaring like a wounded wolf upon his antagonist.

"Leave us," cried Cu Allee, his wrath kindling with his exertions, "leave us, I say, or curp an' dhoul! there will be soon blood enough upon this floor."

"I go, then," said the horseman, perhaps not depending on the sincerity of their promise to stand to him in the quarrel; "but remember, Folling Dearg, that Shane na Shrad's vow of vengeance was never made in vain." And, with that, he departed from the cavern, mounted his steed, and left the trio to their pleasant converse inside.

The moon had now risen over the hills, and gave him light as he pursued his way through a pass on the eastern flank of the mountain he was just about to ascend. At the further extremity of the pass he reined in his horse for a time, to gaze on a scene that opened on his view. Beneath him, in the calm moonlight, and checkered with the remains of an ancient forest, lay the undulating and romantic valley of Cloghanofty, with the dark fort of Castle na Doon rising on a height at one side; and the Oun na Geerait, or River of the Champion, after descending the mountain range opposite the castle, winding in many a silver coil through the low, marshy grounds and indistinct woodlands. Further on, a vista opened between a wood-clad hill on one side, and the ruin-crowned height of Ardpatrick on the other, showing the level plain of Limerick veiled in a light blue mist, through which river and height and castle peered out, like the indistinct and varying panorama of a dream. But what most attracted the attention of the young soldier was a number of fires which glimmered redly upon the lawn that spread before the dark castle beneath him. They were the watch-fires of the cavalry who made their camp here, waiting to join Lord Castlehaven, who was marching at this time, at the head of a well-appointed Irish army, from the county of Tipperary. John of the Bridle, after descending from the pass, entered a small but neatly-kept cottage, at the one end of the straggling village of Fannystown. His mother, a light-haired, good-humoured-looking matron, the daughter of an English settler, stood up as he entered; and, expressing her gladness at his safe return, told a little boy, who sat luxuriously in the corner by the fire, to see after her son's horse.

"Wisha!" said the urchin, with a groan of tribulation, as he went out, "'tis horses, an' horses for ever. I never stopt all day but houldin' horses for them father-long-legs o' cavalthry, an' now I must be at it agin. I liked their prancin' an' gambadin' first well enough, but afther to-day my likin' for it is spilt intirely."

The young soldier sat ruefully by the fire; and turning to his mother, told her of the failure of his search for Alice O'Brien, and of the death of her brother Moran. These were times when death was of but small account in the mind of either man or woman; and John's mother was more apprehensive for the safety of her son than shocked or frightened at the death of his comrade.

"I would wish, John," she said, "that you had long ago given up your mad ideas about that silly wench, Alice. Was it not better that you had taken my advice on the matter, when you could mate better with Amy, Neighbour Holton's daughter?"

"No, mother," said John: "I have the hot Irish blood of my father running in my veins, and I will have full vengeance for the death of my comrade. I have obeyed you in everything else; but ask me not to give up Alice, for it is useless. To-morrow will, I hope, bring me some news of her fate."

The morrow was shining in all the glory of summer up on the woody dells of Fannystown, and the grey hills that towered above them; but with the new day and its many incidents it is better to commence a new chapter.

CHAPTER II.

Until yellow Autumn shall usher the Paschal day,
And Patrick's gay festival come in its train alway;
Until through my coffin the blossoming boughs shall grow,
My love on another I'll never in life bestow.

E. WALSH.

FANNYSTOWN was at this time what is called a protected village; that is, the soldiers of the Government, though often resting there, were not permitted to plunder its inhabitants. It would, however, probably have been plundered and destroyed, had it not been such a convenient resting and camping place, situated as it was in the most dangerous, yet most easily defended, pass between the plains of Cork and Limerick. It consisted of a long line of mud-built houses at one side of the public way; lowly dwellings indeed, but at the same time so thickly planted, that it gave one the notion, when on some important day the inhabitants were astir, of a row of beehives, with all their busy denizens moving to and fro at the commencement of their morning avocations. Behind the village, upon a height, stood the mansion of Sir John Ponsonby, looking down upon the bright waters of the Oun na Geerait—a stream rising in a deep gorge between the mountains, and dancing by many a wild dell and picturesque hollow, until it lost its waters in the rapid Funcheon. The square, loop-holed turrets at the corners of the mansion showed that its owner had not neglected the defence wanted so much in those stormy times; but the rows of bow-windows in the front, facing the stream, gave it a gay appearance, which contrasted strangely with the aspect of its stern neighbour at the other side of the valley—the compact Castle of the Fort; or, as it was named by the surrounding people, Caishla na Doon. This was one of those tall square keeps, so many of which still frown from their rocky sites along the neighbouring plain, telling in their decay, with as much certainty as the pen of the historian, of the troublous times in which they were built, and the domestic habits of the warring races to whom they owed their foundations. It is now considerably increased in dimensions by additions suited to the present day, and has rather a modernized appearance; but part of the original building still remains. At the time of the following events, it was inhabited by Sir Edward Fitzharris, a Catholic gentleman, who, like his neighbour, Sir John Ponsonby, favoured the principles of the Confederation of Kilkenny.

It was high noon when John of the Bridle dashed his horse across the stream, and rode up towards the camp upon the lawn before Castle na Doon.

"Monom! why is she so long, an' the curnil axin for her?" said an old war-worn trooper, who stood guard at the entrance of the camp.

"The news I have to tell him will be likely to set you and your comrades at work, Diarmid," answered John of Bridle. "Here, Jemmy," he continued, addressing a wild, elfish-looking little urchin—the same who had seen to his horse's comfort on the preceding night—"take this bridle, and hold my horse till I come out; and, mind, no galloping this time, for, I fear, the poor fellow will get enough to-day." Jemmy, whose gusto for horse-flesh, notwithstanding his heart-rending complaints on the evening before, was increased with tenfold strength during the morning, took the bridle; and scarcely was the horseman out of sight behind the tents when he was up, like a cat, in the saddle, and careering with unheard-of speed over the lawn.

John of the Bridle entered the castle, and was led by another sentinel up a dark, winding stair into a gloomy-looking chamber, where the colonel, who commanded the cavalry, with a few officers, sat planning busily their future movements.

"The general will be here with the whole army in a few days," said the colonel: "and, on the faith of a soldier! I wish we may see him sooner; for I like not sitting, like a hermit here, when there is so much to be done for our brave fellows. Ha!" continued he, turning to John, as he entered, "here comes our worthy scout; perchance he may inform us how the Burner and his canting vagabonds are preparing for our onslaught. The passes towards St. Leger's den are free for the expedition on to-morrow, young man?"

"The passes are clear enough, colonel; but as I rode yesterday through the forest by Doneraile, a shot from a falconet was near ending my outriding. There are three more on the battlements of St. Leger's Castle, and the walls are thronged with men."

"I trust," rejoined the colonel, "to the broad mouths of our long field-pieces to silence them; but God knows h w. we shall circumvent those rieving villains who yet hang on our march. Hast thou seen that murdering troop that burned the two western hamlets?"

"No, colonel; they are fled towards the Kerry border. Another small troop I saw coming out from Doneraile, and preparing to scour the hills; but they'll meet but a sorry wel come from the wild horsemen of Ballyhoura."

The colonel here took a sealed packet from the table, and put it into the hands of the young horseman. "Thy services," he said, "will merit the reward thou seekest. Deliver this safely to the Governor of Kilmallock, and thou shalt have thy commission as captain of thy troop, and that speedily. I know of no other," said he, addressing the officers, as John of the Bridle was led down stairs by the sentinel,—" I know of none who so marvellously finds his way through those cursed bogs and scroggy passes, and who hath such a goodly share of true courage, as that young man."

As John turned his horse in the direction of Kilmallock, he thought of the events of the preceding day, and how Ellen Roche would bear the news of her lover's death. " But I cannot be at the dance," he said, giving his horse the spur, " if I don't my make way quicker than this."

At the back of Fannystown village was a green in a hollow, through the midst of which ran the Oun na Geerait, after emerging from a narrow, tangled glen at the foot of the mountain. The slope around it was clothed with scattered brushwood; and, where it lost itself in the level space at one side, rose an aged and giant elm-tree, around the trunk of which the villagers, with some of the horsemen from the camp, were thronging to hear the strains of a grey-haired piper, who talked and laughed among them as merrily as if he was in the very heyday of his youth. Around him were gathered the girls and young men of the village, with an occasional trooper, looking for partners, and arranging themselves in two rows, facing each other, in order to commence the *Rinkey-fodha*, or long dance, a figure much resembling the contra-dances of the present day; while outside and half-surrounding the group sat the more aged dwellers of the hamlet; and beyond, upon the green, stood the children in little groups, looking with gleeful and expectant faces for the commencement of the amusements. The long dance was ended, and many an intricate and merry measure danced afterwards by separate groups of four each; at length, a weariness seemed to fall upon them, and they sat around the piper, entreating him to play some of those slow, wild tunes so peculiar to the country. Among the supplicants for the tune was a dark-eyed, young girl, who accompanied her request with so sweet a smile that the old man commenced at once tuning his pipes, with a variety of running notes, which, to the children at least, proved precursors of the most delicious and enchanting melody. This young maiden was Ellen Roche, the betrothed of Moran O'Brien; but who little knew, amid the gladness that reigned around her, of the miseries awaiting her, and of the sad doom of her lover. Her black hair fell in shining masses upon her pretty shoulders, setting off a light and graceful figure, and a sweet face, to which the brilliant and dark eyes gave an expression at once animated and lovely.

"Wirrasthru!" said the piper: "my ould fingers are almost as stiff as that long soord o' Jack Flanagan's there. But everything's stiff, as dhrunken Bill Breen said, when his wife refused to swally a whole barrelful of ale in one dhrink. Well, I had my day out o' the world at any rate." And, so saying, he struck up an ancient Irish march, or war-tune, with such effect that the eyes of the young striplings around him began to sparkle, and even the hands of the wild troopers began to move instinctively towards their sword-hilts; so easily were the rugged and simple natures of those times and scenes moved and excited by the power of the musician.

"Come, an' sit down here by my side, my sweet flower," said he, addressing Ellen Roche, when the war-tune was ended. "Come, an' I'll play up your favourite tune; an' —whisht, ye rantin' divils!—an' you'll sing the ould song I larned you long ago, about the young throoper,—a nater fellow than any o' ye'll ever be anyhow, ye tarin' thieves," he continued, turning to the horsemen. Ellen sat upon the bank beside him; and when the talk was silenced, he commenced to play a singularly sweet old tune, which the young maiden accompanied in a soft and tender voice, with the

words of an Irish ballad, of which the following may be
taken as a translation :—

"JOHNNY DUNLEA.

"There's a tree in the greenwood I love best of all,—
It stands by the side of Easmor's haunted fall,—
For there, while the sunset fell bright far away,
Last I met 'neath its branches my Johnuy Dunlea.

Oh! to see his fine form, as he rode down the hill,
While the red sunlight glowed on his helmet of steel,
With his broadsword and charger, so gallant and gay,
On that evening of woe for my Johnny Dunlea !

He stood by my side; and the love-smile he wore
Still brightens my heart, tho' 'twill beam never more.
'Twas to have but one farewell, then speed to the fray :
'Twas a farewell for ever, my Johnny Dunlea !

For the fierce Saxon soldiers lay hid in the dell,
And burst on our meeting with wild savage yell;
But their dark leader's life-blood I saw that sad day,
And it stained the good sword of my Johnny Dunlea.

My curse on the traitor! my curse on the ball
That stretched my true love by Easmor's haunted fall !
Oh! the blood of his brave heart ebbed quickly away,
And he died in my arms there, my Johnny Dunlea ! "

Alas! little thought the fair singer at the moment, that
her own was a fate like that of the poor maiden of the song.
During the song, had any person looked behind where the
branches of the elm-tree drooped against the slope, they
might have seen a pair of bright, cunning eyes peering out
between the leaves of the copse at the person of the singer.
There was an expression in those weasel eyes that boded no
good to Ellen Roche: but the pair, bright and keen as they
were, had not the fortune to belong to a weasel; they were
the property of a handsome and nimble-looking little man,
who lay upon his breast, gazing thus, but well conceaied
from the observation of the villagers. The moment the song

was ended, and, while the attention of all was taken up in giving the due meed of applause, the little man swung himself cautiously into a projecting branch of the elm-tree; and moving noiselessly along the gnarled limbs, as if he had learned the method from a squirrel, he perched himself for a moment among the thick leaves upon another branch which drooped over the centre of the throng below. Suddenly, he let himself drop into the midst of the circle; and, before any one knew how he had come there, he had performed half a dozen "summersets" upon the green.

"Theige na Meerval! Theige na Meerval!" cried the delighted children.

"Theige na Meerval himself!" exclaimed their elders. "Honom an' dhoul! but I believe he's after fallin' out o' the sky."

"Thundher-an-ages, no!" said a trooper. "Doesn't every mother's sowl o' ye know that he's invisible when he ikes, an' can walk invisible into the centre o' people; an' wid one touch make himself be seen agin by every person, in one morthial minnit?"

"I did fall out o' the sky," said the Man of Wonders, at the same time cutting a few capers that blended their surprise with immense merriment. "Where is the use in me bein' enchanted, if I cannot circumvint myself into a blast o' wind when I likes?"

The strains of the poor piper were now neglected; and all thronged around the showman—for that was his particular and favourite profession—and began to press still closer, with open mouths, and faces of wonder and expectancy. Na Meerval now took a strangely-made knife from his pocket, and commenced to show off some of his feats. Suddenly he stooped till his face almost touched the ground; and, amidst innumerable "Monoms!" "Dhar Dias!" and "Hiernas!" from the astonished bystanders, jerked himself up straight again, with the blade of the knife sticking upwards through his tongue. He now beckoned for more space; and, when he found sufficient, he stooped forward, with his hands resting on the ground, and, springing over, stood upon his feet again, holding the knife aloft in his hand.

"Ha, ha!" he exclaimed, "if all o' ye used your knives that way, maybe 'tis little soft talk ye'd be able to give the girls afterwards. Did ye ever hear where I wint the first time I made myself invisible? Divil a place would plaise me but Spain, to larn magic from an ould anshint theif, that was as great as two pickpockets with the Ould Oganach * himself. He could see me when no one else could; an' I stopt with him 'till the murtherin' ould thief turned me away out of invy, when he saw I was batin' out himself. Howsomdever, I'll show ye somethin' that he larned me." And, so saying, he raised his hand, and apparently, to his audience, struck himself lightly on the mouth. A volume of bluish smoke, accompanied with bright sparks, issued suddenly from between his open jaws; at the appearance of which the spectators, so delighted were they at the marvel, set up a wild shout of applause and wonder.

"There is one thing howsomdever," said he again, "that every person bates me at,—gamin'." And, walking to a smooth stone, which served for a seat, he drew from his pocket a dice-box and laid it beside him. "Now," continued he, turning to the troopers, at the same time laying two silver coins upon the stone, "ye were paid not long ago, an' here is a flamin' fine time to make the forthin' of every livin' sowl among ye."

"I made my forthin' once in the sackin' of a town an' lost agin every jingler of it in battle; an' now gamin' won't re-make it for me," said a huge, stern-looking trooper, with the marks of a great sword-cut across his face.

"Well, purshuin' to me, do you hear that?" said a jolly, careless fellow, who was already seated by Na Meerval's side,

* The Devil.

with the dice-box rattling in his hand, and his stake down :
" Mun Callaghan, that would sell himself to a certain curious
gintleman undhernathe us, body an' bones an' sowl, for money,
sayin' now there is no varthue in gamin'!" so saying he
threw and won. This good fortune made others eager for
the play, till, after various games, most of the troopers found
the few coins they possessed since the last pay-day comfortably
transferred to the pockets of Na Meerval. He now turned
to Mun Callaghan.

" You see I'm richer now than when I began. Come an'
larn the sweet an' inchantin' mystheries o' the dice-box.
Play, man, play ; an,' as you're so fond o' the money, maybe
you'd win it all back again."

" I will not play," answered Mun, in an angry tone.

" Yerrah! man, can't you take one chance?" said his
comrades. " The devil resave the much we're at a loss
anyhow; for, like yourself, 'tis little we had to lose. Ructions
to us, man! why dont you play ?"

" Bekaise I have an' ould an' wake mother beyont the
hills, wid no one to purtect her, an' who wants what I can
give her out o' my pay—not to have me loose in gamin',"
answered Mun bitterly. This produced a laugh among the
more careless of his comrades; and the Man of Wonders,
emboldened by the merriment, overstepped seemingly his
usual cautiousness.

" Yerrah!" said he, "maybe 'twas batin' you with a sthraw
or a rish for your conthriary doins your ould mother was
that put that tattherin' glin of wound acrass your face."
The answer was a blow from the ponderous fist of Mun,
which sent Na Meerval spinning, like a cork, along the green.
The blow, however, certainly stunned him somewhat less
than he pretended.

" Oh!" said he, as if waking from a deadly swoon, and still
lying extended on the grass, " I'm done in airnest at last—
kilt unnathrally. Here is my brain spinnin' round an' round,

like a wheel-o'-forthin,'—the rale sign o' death. Oh!"
And he sank apparently into a swoon again, while the villagers gathered round him in instant commiseration of his hard
fate. "Is there any good Christhian," he exclaimed, reviving
once more—"is there any good an' charitable Christhian that
would lade me to their home till I die in pace? My brain!
my brain! Lade me up to Moureen Roche's, the ould widow o'
the hollow, where I often slept before. Is that Ellen Roche
I see? Lade me, up a *colleen dhas*, 'till I die in pace."

He now stood up, but tottered; and Ellen Roche, coming
forward, caught him by the arm, and, assisted by one of the
young men, began to lead him up to where her mother's
house stood in a lonely hollow some distance up the glen.
After going a few perches, Na Meerval seemed to get somewhat
stronger, and told the young man that he could reach the
house with the help of Ellen Roche. The young man,
possessed altogether with the idea of his sweetheart,
whom he saw looking with a jealous eye after, turned back
willingly, just as Mun Callaghan, with many a reproach
ringing in his ears, was stalking off towards the camp. The
incident was, however, soon forgotten in a short time, and
the dance renewed as merrily as ever.

In the meantime, Ellen Roche, with Na Meerval behind
her, led the way towards her home, till they reached a
lonely spot where the path crossed the glen; and here, instead of dying in peace as he promised, the Man of Wonders
sprang at the unsuspecting girl, and, before she could scream
for help, tied a kerchief round her face, which rendered her
unable either to see or call for assistance. He now gave a
low whistle; and, at the signal, his two comrades of the
cave stepped out from a dark nook in the side of the glen.
Ellen Roche, unlike the majority of heroines, did not faint
at once, but, like the brave girl that she was, resisted to the
utmost the efforts of the three, as they bore her through the
forest towards the pass leading between the mountains, till,

at length, entirely exhausted, she sank into a passive kind of
stupor, in which she continued until the kerchief was taken
off her face.

On opening her eyes, she found herself in a narrow recess
between two rocks, which, by way of rendering it habitable,
was roofed with boughs of oak, and thatched over with
bundles of heath and fern. It was situated on the side of a
deep glen, through which the bright bog-tinted stream rushed
downward with a hollow murmur; and its entrance opened
towards a wide moor, whose undulating expanse stretched
out, drear and lonely, until it terminated in a low range of
dark hills to the west. Outside the door of the hut, the eyes
of the young girl fell upon two objects, each remarkable in its
appearance, but from the possession of very different qualities.
One has been described before : it was no other than Cu
Allee, standing guard at the entrance; and the other was the
most beautiful whitethorn ever seen by human eyes, growing
on the extremity of a green tongue of land at the opposite
side of the glen. It shot up in a single stem to about seven
feet from the ground, and then branched into three graceful
arms which extended themselves from side to side, in ramifi-
cations so singularly light and beautiful that the wild inhabitants
of the mountains should not be deemed over-credulous for believing that the fairies trained its sprays—upon which some
white blossoms still lingered—to assume those lovely forms;
and that they made the little green around it one of their
most favoured retreats.

But, if Ellen Roche was surprised for an instant at the
beauty of the whitethorn, it was with dismay and terror
that she gazed on the uncouth form of Theige the Wolf, whom
she mistook—no great mistake indeed—for one of those
wild spirits, who, in the shape of little red men, are believed
by the Irish to haunt lonely places among the mountains,
and whose appearance is a sure sign of the speedy doom of
the unfortunate person who beholds them. She looked upon

him for an instant; and, on noticing the evil expression of
his eyes, covered her face with her hands, and sank, in the
extremity of her terror, on a stone seat which lay beside
her.   Cu Allee noticed her dismay; and, although it did not
at all advance her in his good graces, he did not hate her as
he did every one else, for he began to imagine some resemblance between her and his young sister, whom he had laid
not long ago in the old churchyard of Doneraile.   In fact,
in thinking of his sister, the only person for whom he ever
felt anything like affection, he began to cast about in his
mind why he stood guard there upon a poor girl in whom he
recognized a similarity of appearance, and to picture to himself how he would feel, after doing one good action, by
effecting her liberation.   It was with him as with all who have
turned on the evil path through life.   The human heart, in
its innocence, is like a lovely bower, where the virtues, with
their fair train of good and beautiful thoughts, make their
dwelling; but, when the devil once gets possession of the
keys, out go the virtues and their bright attendants, and,
though they return frequently, and knock and knock for
admittance, the stern answer of the evil demon inside scares
them off, like a flock of white doves at the yell of the
mountain eagle.   By-and-bye the demon hides the keys, the
bower withers and becomes rotten; and the virtues, led by
our good angel, go searching, searching, but, alas! rarely
find the means of entrance to make it bloom again.   The
spirit of evil, in order to expel the good intention on this
occasion from the breast of Cu Allee, thought fit to send a
delegate in the person of the Man of Wonders, who, advancing
up the glen, whispered something into the ear of the dwarf,
at which he quitted his post, and proceeded with wonderful
agility up the mountain at the back of the hut.   Na Meerval
entered, but paused for a time inside the door when he found
himself unnoticed by Ellen Roche, who, with her face
buried in her mantle, sat still in the same position as

when she retired on seeing Theige the Wolf. At length he spoke :—

"Yerrah! my dark flower o' the mountains, is'nt it unnathral to see you sittin' that way, as bronach an' sorrowful as if all belongin' to you were laid out, an' the wake-candles burnin' over them ?"

Ellen sat up, for she knew the voice. "An' is it you," she said, "you black-hearted villain, that spakes to me in such a way, after taking me away from my poor mother, whose heart, I know, is broke at the news already ? Let me go, I say." And she gathered her mautle around her, and prepared to dart from the door. "Let me go, or 'twont be long till some one you know will have his heavy revenge on you for this day's work."

"Fair an' aisy, Misthress Ellen," said Na Meerval, putting her gently back to her seat. "Listen to a few words I have to say, an' 'twill make you a little kindher."

"I can't listen to anything but about my laving this. You know you often got food an' shelter an' kindness in my mother's house, an' this is not the way to pay back those who ever au' always helped you in your need."

"That very shelther an' kindness was my desthruction; for, from the first night I slept undher your roof, I fell in love—you know with whom—an' 'tis conshumin' my heart to cinders ever since. Listen to me for a minnit. There is one you think that's dhramin' o' you, mornin', noon, and night. I know him, of coorse. But I tell you that Moran O'Brien has stopt thinkin' o' you since yesterday; so, if he promised to do so always, he's false to his word. Take the love, then, of a truer man, who'll stick to you through life an' death."

"It is false," answered Ellen vehemently. "Moran is still true to me, an' will be as true to his revenge upon you, if you don't let me away."

"You don't know me, Ellen Roche. Thrue or false, you'll never have him for a husband, nor have no one else either, barrin' myself. I tell you he'll never think on you more; an' look at this," said he, at the same time drawing a small silver cross from his bosom, "if he was true in his heart and soul, would he let a purty-faced crathure, nearly as nate as myself, take this from round his neck? Upon this blessed cross, taken from the neck of a false man, who never more can see you, I swear to love you through pace an' war, an' through life an' death, for ever an' ever."

Ellen looked at the cross. It was Moran's. She had herself placed it round his neck; and he, poor fellow! had vowed at the same time that he would never part with it but in death. Suddenly the thought flashed upon her mind that he was dead—murdered by Na Meerval and his accomplices. She looked instinctively at the sword by Na Meerval's side. It was Moran's. The horrible reality burst at once upon her mind; and, with a piercing and agonizing shriek, she sank senseless on the floor of the hut.

On awakening from her swoon, she found herself lying upon some soft heath in another apartment. A wooden vessel filled with water lay beside her upon a flat stone, with some bread. This she was enabled to observe by a few streams of red light which darted inwards through the chinks of an old wooden door which separated the recess in which she lay from the outer one. She cautiously arose, and looking through one of the chinks, saw Na Meerval and his two comrades sitting round a heap of blazing wood in the apartment she had occupied on the preceding evening; for it was now far advanced in the night. She turned round in silent misery and fear, and, sinking her face once more in the folds of her mantle, sat in her despair until another morning was shining gloriously over the grey summits and deep valleys that surrounded her.

CHAPTER III.

I buckled on my armour,
　　And my sword so keen and bright;
I took my gallant charger,
　　And I rode him to the fight.
We met the foeman early,
　　Beside yon castle hoar,
And slew them àll by tower and wall,
　　And by the dark lake-shore.
　　　　　　　　　　BALLAD.

ABOUT sunrise that morning John of the Bridle took his way up the gorge through which poor Ellen had been borne. He had returned from Kilmallock on the previous evening, after delivering the despatch, and joined the dancers on the green of Fannystown. On inquiring for Ellen Roche, he was told the incident that had occurred, and of Ellen's accompanying Na Meerval to her home. Suspecting some unfair dealing on the part of Na Meerval, he proceeded directly to the house of Maureen Roche; but she could give no account of her daughter, except that she had gone early in the day to the dance. The alarm was given, and every place searched, even the cave where John of the Bridle met the three Timothys; but no trace of the young girl could be found. John of the Bridle was on horseback most of that night, and, after sending some of his friends in other directions, took his way at sunrise up the gorge that led between the hills. On reaching the highest point of a craggy ridge, he directed his course over a wide and elevated moorland, strewn irregularly with huge masses of rock. Riding for some time in a southerly directiou, he at length reached where the barren moorland merged into the stunted copsewood of the upland forest; and here he was met by a lathy and light-footed *gorsoon* whom he accosted.

" Rody," said he, "where is Remy of the Glen and the horseman ?"

" They're below, in the ould castle o' Kilcolman, captin ; but come on down to 'em, for they're in riglar currywhibes. about somethin', an' wantin' you badly."

When they had proceeded for some time through the forest, Rody. stopped. "There, captin, is the ould castle beyant there ; an' here is the glin, fwhare all the horses are left for me to mind. So come down now, captin, an' let me put your horse wid the rest."

John of the Bridle dismounted, and, guided by Rody, led his horse to a deep hollow in the forest, with bushy precipices all round it ; and here, feeding upon heaps of dried grass, stood between forty and fifty horses, accoutred, and ready for their owners. Leaving his horse among them to the care of Rody, John proceeded quickly along the forest pathway, until, at length, he stood before the ruined outworks of Kilcolman. Here he was met by a short, dark man, who stood as sentinel by the broken gate, and who told him to go in at once, for those inside were impatiently expecting him. On entering the dilapidated doorway, before him opened an arch-roofed and gloomy apartment, the principal hall of the castle, lit by a great fire of blazing wood ; which, as the chimney and windows were all stopped up, filled the whole space inside with a thick cloud of smoke. Around the fire, in various attitudes, talking, laughing, and eating, were congregated about twenty men—some of the owners of the horses. The fire blazed and crackled, its red flame lighting up the wild visages of the horsemen, and glinting with picturesque effect on the half-polished arms that strewed the floor, or lay against the craggy wall. One young man, turning round, saw John of the Bridle, or the Captain, as they called him ; for it was he that always led them on their wild forays.

" Arrah, blur-an-ages ! here is the captin himself, at the

very time we wanted him," exclaimed the young man. "I bleeve 'twas the Good People themselves that sent him." `

"'Twas not, then, Shamus, but the very worst of people that sent me here. But why are ye sitting thus? and what account have ye of the troops that came out from Doneraile?"

"First an' foremost, captain," said Remy of the Glen—a tall, young fellow, the boldest and merriest-looking of them all, and who, from the respect paid to his opinions by his comrades, appeared to have the command in the absence of John of the Bridle—"First an' foremost, we're waitin to know would you come; an' second, we have a plan made out among ourselves that'll maybe settle with them throopers—for they're now comin' over the hills back to Doneraile—better than if we met them on the hills; an'—*aur vonom!*—'twill give us what we had'nt this many a day—a little sport. Twenty o' the boys are now lyin' in ambush outside in the wood, an' five or six more over on the height; an' the very minnit that the throopers get a look at them, they're to run back here, an' never stir out o' this till the Black Captain begins to smoke them out. Dhar Dhia! when we ketch himself an' his throopers among these ould thraps o' walls, but I'll soon have a betther helmet than this rusty ould grissid on my head at present!"

John of the Bridle was strategist enough to see that this was an excellent plan for settling accounts with the troopers. The only improvement he would suggest was that he should go himself, and head the ambuscade. He found the men outside crouched among the thick underwood of the forest, and waiting with impatience for the coming of their enemies. In the meantime, those who served for a decoy sat upon the summit of a steep height, looking westward upon a troop of about thirty horsemen, returning from their murdering expedition. Suddenly one of the troopers looked up, and, beholding the wild-looking figures on the summit, pointed them out to his leader, the Black Captain; who, sticking his

long spurs into his horse's flanks, dashed towards them, followed by his men. Away rushed the others, making a circuit
in order to avoid the hollow where the horses were concealed,
and were just in among their comrades when the troopers
appeared in front of the castle upon the shore of the lake.

"Ha, ha!" exclaimed one of them, as he entered, "we
have the bloody murtherers caught at last, an', by the morthial
big soord o' Brian Boru, but they have nate horses!"

All inside now arose, and stood darkly around Remy of
the Glen, their arms flashing in the red firelight, and the glow
of revenge and hate shining in the wild countenances as they
listened for the onset of their enemies. Remy now looked
out, and beheld through the shattered outworks the troopers
in a cluster by the lake, apparently deliberating on the best
method of capturing the fugitives of the castle. Among them
stood Theige the Wolf, like an evil spirit, grinning with glee
at the prospect of the exercise he was apparently to have in
his darling profession of a skibbioch, or hangman. The
Black Captain now gave some orders, at which they all dismounted; and one of them, a low-sized, lank-visaged, but
stout man, who went by the euphonious name of Corporal
Ebenezer Kick-the-Goad, advanced. to the gateway of the
castle.

"Come forth," he exclaimed, ye robbing Amalekites, or
ye shall die the death of wolves, whom ye imitate, betaking
yourselves to dens and caverns to avoid the path of the just
and chosen!"

The answer was a couple of bullets from the inside, one
of which stretched him by the gate, wounding him severely;
the other breaking the leg of the Black Captain's horse, which
stood on the shore almost in a direct line behind him.

"Now, by the soul of Abraham!" said the captain, "They
shall die. Follow me, children of Zion, and we'll send their
souls from yon unhallowed den to get an eternal taste of the
punishments awaiting God's accursed."

All now advanced towards the gateway, firing as they went, their shots killing a few inside. The besieged, on their part, were not idle; for, as the troopers came clambering up the gateway, and through the rugged apertures of the outworks, they were saluted by a volley from the doorway which killed several of them, and sent the Black Captain rolling over and over in his death agony almost down to the shore of the lake. Finding their reception a little too hot, the rest retreated behind the shelter of the walls, in order to get time for a little deliberation before they renewed the attack.

"That's my shot," said Remy of the Gleu, when he saw the Black Captain rolling down; "an' his helmet an' back-an-breast are mine. Poor Randal Breen, that broke the horse's leg outside, has no claim; for he's shot himself."

The command of the besiegers now devolved upon a gigantic, iron-visaged man, the tallest of the troop, who, as he said himself, had cast away as an unhallowed thing his name of the flesh, but amply recompensed himself by taking the tremendous appellation of Habakkuk Burn-the-Gentiles. This changing of names was the universal custom of the Puritans of those days. Burn-the-Gentiles held the rank of sergeant, and was an experienced and courageous soldier. The ambuscade had not yet come out from their hiding-place, and it is necessary to explain the reason. The Black Captain, on picketing the horses, had left them in care of Cu Allee and the Rev. Hezekiah Shout-the-Word-from-Zion; who, although a preacher of the Word, was perhaps one of the keenest-eyed soldiers of the troop. At the moment of the first attack, the ambuscade, therefore, could not by any possibility come unawares on their enemies. Various methods were suggested by the troopers for dislodging the besieged, but Burn-the-Gentiles at length proposed one which was universally acceded to.

"Comrades in the chosen path," he said, "the cunning of

the Amoritish slaves have prevailed for the moment. But it
shall avail them not. Even as Samson burned the vineyards,
so shall we burn to death those children of sin in yon accursed
house. Depart. Gather ye fern and the dried grass of the
forest, and place it even as a burning and suffocating and
scorching barrier before the door of the heathen."

This order was obeyed with such alacrity that they soon
had a great heap of half-withered boughs, grass, and fern,
piled up beside the outer wall. Of this, each took a portion;
and, stealing round the corners of the castle, they threw their
bundles from them into the door-way, and in a short time
had the whole space filled up with combustibles ready for
the igniting spark. The heap was now set on fire and all
thronged around—even the Reverend Hezekiah himself coming up from the horses to be a witness—and stood in immense
satisfaction at the idea of the sport they were to have in the
charitable work of roasting half-a-dozen of their fellow-crea-
tures; and so intent were they on the interesting operation,
that they never noticed the approach of a body of men
equalling themselves in number, which, led by John of the
Bridle, came slowly but surely to the attack behind
them. On came these vengeful men, stealing like panthers
approaching their prey. Suddenly, with a savage yell, they
sprang upon the rear of the terrified troopers; and at the
same moment the burning heath was scattered, as by the
blast of a tempest, from the doorway, and out rushed Remy
of the Glen and his remaining followers. Shot after shot
rang around the ancient castle, shout and groan and sabre-
clash woke the sullen echoes of the lake: but, after some
moments, a few groans, scarcely louder than the murmur of
the waves against the shore, fell upon the ear; for all the
troopers, except Burn-the-Gentiles, Shout-the-Word-from-
Zion, and a few others with equally astounding appellations,
met their death in that wild onset. The horse of John of
the Bridle, hearing the shots, broke loose from the guardian-

ship of Rody, and darted down to the scene of conflict. John sprang upon his back, and, with a few others, who had each appropriated a trooper's horse, galloped away in pursuit of the fugitives, while the remainder of his men rushed after the chargers of the other dead troopers, which were careering in all directions around Lough Ullair. On riding somewhat more than a mile in pursuit of Burn-the-Gentiles, who had turned in a different direction from his comrades, John of the Bridle reined in his horse; for the redoubtable sergeant fled with such reckless rapidity through the forest that it was quite useless to pursue him any farther.

In the mean time, John's men had secured the horses, and brought them in; and were now crowded in the front of the castle, dividing the spoils of their fallen enemies. Some of their own comrades had also fallen, their bodies lying side by side with those of the troopers. In the absence of their captain, Remy was necessarily the umpire; and it was amusing to see with what tact and rapidity he managed the affair. Putting aside the horses to be disposed of according to the judgment of John of the Bridle, he first cast away his own old rusty helmet, and arrayed himself in the bright morion and corselet of the Black Captain; then, to one of his men he gave a back-and-breast, to another a sword and belt, and to some one else a helmet, and so on, until the whole spoil was disposed of in a satisfactory manner.

Whilst engaged in admiring themselves in their new habiliments, they heard a shriek behind them; and, on turning round, beheld Alice O'Brien running towards them, pursued by a tall, dark woman, who seemed blind with fury, for she still came on quite unheeding the threatening gestures of Remy and his comrades. Remy ran towards Alice, who fell fainting into his arms; and a few others laid hold on her pursuer, who struggled and kicked and bit in their grasp with all the energy of a demon. Alice and the woman were still in the apartment described in the beginning of the first chapter, when the castle was suddenly occupied by Remy of the Glen and his companions. Not knowing who were beneath them, they had remained hidden during the morning. Then came the noise of the fighting, the silence, and the distribution of the spoils; and Alice, hearing her cousin Remy's voice, could bear the suspense no longer; so, darting suddenly out through a ruined window, she clambered down the old broken wall, pursued by the woman, and was thus happily restored to her friends. The old woman now seemed calmed a little in her fury; but, in all the varieties of abuse that the human tongue is capable of, she commenced to demonstrate to her captors that she was not at all afraid of them, or anything they could do.

"Take the ould bird o' Satin into the castle, an' roast her like a throut, upon the fire," said one of the horsemen.

"Tie her to one o' the horse's tails, the ould banshee, and let him whip, like a thimble-man, through the forest wid her," exclaimed another.

"No," said Remy, "let her go her own ways. We have got plenty of her already." And, with that, she was liberated; and, leaving Alice and the horseman, with many a curse upon her tongue, she walked off round the lake, and took her way in the direction of Doneraile.

CHAPTER IV

" But oh! one morn I clomb a hill,
To sigh alone, to weep my fill,
And there Heaven's mercy sent to me
My treasure rare, Ben—Erinni!"
                                        IRISH BALLAD.

REINING up from the pursuit of Burn-the-Gentiles, John of the Bridle dismounted in a deep hollow of the forest, in order to fasten a strap of his armour which had become loosened in the fray. On sheathing his sword, and while in the act of buckling the strap, he was seized around the body and arms as if in the grasp of a giant, and dashed roughly on his back to the ground. And it was truly a giant; for, on looking up, the young horseman beheld Theige of the Red Cloak standing over him, with an expression of triumphant hate in his massive features, and his skean in his hand, ready to prevent his victim from making any movement of escape. John instinctively moved his hand to where his sword ought to have been; but the belt had been unbuckled when he was grasped first, and sword and dagger thrown to a distance from where he lay. Just at this moment, the attention of both was attracted to another object. It was Cu Allee, who had made his escape from battle, and who now, darting from the thicket, was instantly clinging, like a catamount, to the saddle of John's charger. The horse, not at all relishing this companionship, commenced rearing and dashing wildly up and down the hollow, till at length, by means of an agile spring to one side and a demivolt, he landed his rider in the bottom of a rough, gravelly drain. Up started Cu Allee with a shrill yell of vengeance, and all bleeding from the fall; and, with his long dagger gleaming in his hand, rushed after the horse, which, clearing the thicket at the verge of the hollow, gained the more open part of the forest, and was soon safe from the resentment of his pursuer. Folling Dearg turned again to his prostrate companion.

"Ha, ha!" he almost yelled, with a savage laugh of triumph, "hur is caught at last. Dhar Vurrhia! but it was like a riffinly little dog follyin' on the thrack of a wild wolf. An' a dog's death Shrane na Shrad must die for that sore blow in the cave, an' for crossing Theige Folling Dearg in his love." And so saying, he made John of the Bridle arise and march off in the direction of the Fairy Whitethorn; Folling Dearg keeping close behind, with a short gun ready pointed in his hand; and Cu Allee closer still, his dagger reaory to be plunged into the back of their captive, should he make any hostile movement.

During the early part of that day, a burst of gay sunshine had flooded hill and valley ; but, as the morning advanced, the sky was overstrewn by layers of dull, copper-coloured clouds, which came moving up from the eastern horizon with the slowness and regularity of a well-disciplined army proceeding to battle. Not a breeze stirred the leaves on the thickets ; and a dead and oppressive silence reigned around, which was at length broken by a low, rumbling sound behind the distant mountains. A sudden flash now illuminated the far-off horizon. It was succeeded by others, which, as they came, traversed a wider arch of the heavens, and by thunder, each successive peal waxing louder and more hollow, till the very earth seemed bursting behind the hills. At length, and just as Timothy of the Red Cloak and his ill-favoured companion, with their captive, were descending the side of a bare mountain, a bright ball of electric fire burst from the bosom of a black mass of cloud on the summit, and, darting in a zigzag course along the sky, burst, overspreading the whole wide arch with a flood of blinding and intense brillancy. Then came a dead silence, only broken by the patter of a few heavy rain-drops, which was succeeded by an explosion so loud and hollow that the very rocks seemed tottering from their firm foundations. A black column of falling rain, like a waterspout, now advanced up the eastern heights, and spread and spread till the dark moorland and steep valley were one universal hiss and clatter of falling drops.

Unstayed for a moment by the gloom and loud deluging of the storm, John of the Bridle and his captors proceeded over the bogs till they reached the edge of the deep glen through which the Ounanar, now swelled into a great torrent, rushed downward on the rocks, whirling along its jagged banks with a roar that almost drowned the frequent reverberations of the thunder overhead. Before them the stream was too deep and violent to attempt a passage across ; so they proceeded upwards some distance to the junction of its two branches, where its bed was broader, and, consequently, more shallow. Here they changed their order of march, and began to wade the torrent, Folling Dearg in front of the captive, and Cu Allee close behind, with his long dagger still glittering in his hand. Close above them the two streams rushed into one, forming a black and boiling pool, whose waters, as if eager for more noisy strife, issuing out, foamed and hissed and roared hoarsely around the many fragments of rock that obstructed their way to the narrow and torn channel some distance below. The three were now past the middle of the torrent. A bright blaze of lightening for an instant illuminated the gloomy valley, when, with almost the suddenness of the electric flash, John of the Bridle turned round, snatched his sword-belt from the shoulders of Cu Allee, and dashed headlong downward into the whirling current. That wild current, re-inforced by some roaring tributary, now rose with fearful suddenness, higher and higher, till it became too powerful for mortal strength to contend against ; so the disappointed pair, after a few unsuccessful plunges, were fain to scramble to the bank before them, and leave John of the Bridle to the flood, which they supposed would dash him to pieces against the rocks beneath them in the glen. But the sudden swell saved him ; for, just as he was about to be shot downward through the narrow channel, he was raised high enough to catch at the naked roots of a giant ash-tree which grew upon the edge of the bank. With a mighty effort he heaved himself upward, and clutched one of these; scrambled higher still, and stood all blinded by the yellow foam upon the bank where they first looked for a ford across the torrent. At length he turned round, and shook his sword at the two, as they stood beneath the cliffs at the opposite side. For answer to his defiance, a bullet from the musketoon of Folling Dearg whistled across the glen and struck with a shrill clang upon his breastplate, but, unable to penetrate the good steel, glanced aside, striking off the head of a sapling that grew hard-bye. Little relishing another visitor like this, John of the Bridle struck upwards through the wood; and, on gaining the open heath, took his way in the direction of the spot where he was made prisoner that morning.

After crossing a high, plashy bog, he began to ascend a stone-strewn hill, on whose summit rose a cairn—probably an ancient landmark, or some monumental heap, erected long ago over some chief who had fallen in battle among the hills. The rain now began to abate, and, as he stood beside the cairn, had ceased altogether. He sat himself upon a fragment of stone, and looked around. Beneath him, towering over the green forest, lay Kilcolman Castle. Between him and the skirts of the forest spread a slanting rushy moorland, across which a body of horsemen were now advancing, whom, notwithstanding the distance, he instantly knew to be his own comrades. As they drew nearer, he could distinguish that one horse was without a rider, and that a female, seated behind a horseman, came on in the front of the cavalcade. Without waiting to see more, he now set off across the moor, as quickly as he could, towards a deep glen, which he knew was to be crossed by his compauions. He and they coming to opposite sides of the glen at the same time, they soon observed him, and gave a wild and glad shout of recognition; on which, the led horse, breaking away from the rider that held him, dashed down across the glen, and, with many a gladsome neigh, came bounding towards the spot where John of the Bridle stood. It was his own steed. After escaping from Cu Allee, he was caught by Rody, in the forest, and brought in with the other horses. But a far more welcome surprise now awaited John. The party had crossed the glen, and were close upon him, when the female sprang lightly from behind Remy of the Glen, and the next moment John of the Bridle was clasping fondly to his breast his long-lost and long-sought love, Alice O'Brien. **As the** wild horsemen circled round, and surveyed the meeting of the lovers, their rugged countenances lit up with pleasure; and each began to tell, with many rough oaths and contradictions, how and where they had rescued Alice.

"Arrah, by the holy staff o' the saint!" exclaimed Remy of the Glen, "but if we're not real fortunate men! There I was this mornin', with a bare breast, an' an ould rusty pot of a helmet; an' here I am now with the black ould Parliaminther's back-an'-breast, an' a helmet as bright as the flamin' diamond o' Lough Lein. But what is it all to the bringin' back o' my sweet cousin Alice into the arms of our captain, her own true an' dear lover, as she says herself? I'll bet my new helmet against Jack Burke's ould spurs that I'll grind the flags of any floor to smithereens, dancin' at their weddin'!" And, with that, he turned his spurs inward, and, in the excess of his delight, commenced driving his horse in an infinite number of capers and gambadoes around the splashing bog.

"Little you knew, John," said Alice, after they had mutually told the sorrow each felt during the time they were separated, "little you knew, when speaking to Theige of the Red Cloak about restoring me, that it was he and his men b re ne away into the hills. They stole upon me that evening at the milking bawn in Glenisheen, and took me first to his hut beside the Fairy Whitethorn. The black traitor! did he think that I could give my heart to such as he—a betrayer among his own companions, and to his native country? When he found it all in vain, he took me away to Kilcolman, and left me with his sister, to sell me to the Black Captain—he who, they tell me, lies beyond there by the wall of the castle. But I am rescued; and now, my dearest John, we meet, I hope, to part no more."

Leaving John and Alice to their happy thoughts, it is time to return to Folling Dearg and his sweet-faced com-

panion. They made no attempt to pursue their captive, for
the simple reason that it was impossible for them to cross
the flood; but, turning upwards along the edge of the glen,
they soon reached their hut, opposite the whitethorn. In its
outer apartment Theige na Meerval was sitting before them;
and, to judge by the expression of his countenance, he
seemed in no very elysian humour. They stood silent for
some time, the face of each indicating, in its own peculiar
manner, the dark passions aroused by disappointment. Na
Meerval was the first to break it :—

"Cu Allee's work is over, is it? An' why didn't you
bring Shane na Shrad here, as you promised, an' let him
take his last swing from the anch of the whitethorn outside? Or maybe he escaped yo. Ha! you said this mornin'
that your revinge was so strong that you could scent Shane
na Shrad's footsteps thro' coom an' forest, wherever he
went."

"My curse upon this roarin' flood undher us!" exclaimed
Folling Dearg, "when we were crossin,' an so far that we
could'nt get back here agin, it, I may say, took him in its
arms, an' tore him from between us, an' threw him safe upon
the bank we left. An' he's gone. My black an' heavy an'
burnin' curses upon him, night, noon, and mornin'!"

"Yes: Cu Allee's work!" said that worthy: "why didn't
you do the work you got for yourself? There is a difference between bringin' a strong man across a floody river,
and coming round the colleen you have inside there. I
thought ye'd be in love with each other in a minnit. Why
did'nt you do that work with your sleight-o'-hand?"

"I'll do it yet," answered the little man, in all the
energy of vindictive passion; "an' if I can't," continued he,
laying his hand upon his dagger, "there's some sleight-o'-hand
in this, an' I'll make it help me, an' be my matchmaker."

"If I'd depended upon my skean, an' not upon Cu
Allee's gad," said Folling Dearg, " my mortal inimy would'nt

D

be walkin' free across the mountains this blessed hour. But
maybe he isn't gone far yet. The flood will soon begin to
go down; give us somethin' to ate, an' we'll see what revinge
can do to overtake him."

After partaking of some black, coarse bread, and making a few other preparations, they crossed the flood once
more, and set out again in pursuit of John of the Bridle.

When something more than an hour had passed, Na
Meerval rolled away the large stone with which the door of
the inner apartment was fastened, and stood once more in the
presence of Ellen Roche.

"Come!" said he sternly, "this is my third an' last time
for askin' you. Say you'll have me, love or no love, an'
your troubles are over."

Ellen had tried every kind of entreaty before. She now
determined to brave it out, and meet her fate, if it came to
the worst, as fearlessly as she could.

"I said that but once in my life, an' you know to whom:
can I say it now to one of the murderers of my betrothed
Moran?"

"Your betrothed! He's betrothed to the worms by this,
an' what's the use o' thinkin' about him any longer? Think
o' the long life that's before you, an' that you must spend it
in my company, whether you like it or not. Think o' the
fair journeys, an' pleasant days, an' fine dresses, you'll have
when my wife, an' forget your betrothed for a truer man. I
ask again. Say but that you'll have me, an' we'll leave the
company of Folling Dearg an' Cu Allee, an' fly to a more
peaceful land, where we can live together happy."

"I think," rejoined Ellen, "of the life that was before
me, and that you have blasted for ever. I think of him
who lies in some bloody nook, with none to pray for him,
and none to cover him from the ravens an' the wild wolves
of the hills. I think of all this; and, if I live, each day
your life will be near the brink, while I am near you. Keep

me, then, if you dare; an' see how I'll remember the long
life before me!"

The Man of Wonders saw that any further picturing of
a pleasant life in his company to Ellen was useless. His
demeanour now changed with a startling suddenness. As a
connected set of machinery with its complicated wheels,
when one important spring is put out of order, whirls round,
and runs into irretrievable confusion and destruction, so,
when one passion is set completely loose, a host of others is
aroused to help its madness. And it was so with Na Meerval.
His vindictive eyes, and every lineament of his face seemed
lighted up and blazing with the anger of disappointed love,
if his could be called love; and the revenge that knows no
mercy was but too truly shown in the iron grasp with which
he clutched his dagger, as he drew it to strike at the defence-
less bosom of poor Ellen Roche. But, the moment he
raised his dagger, he was struck from behind himself,
on the head, and with a force that stretched him swooning
on the floor.

Accustomed as Na Meerval was to produce wonders the
most amazing, he was not at all prepared for the miraculous
change of circumstances that presented itself to his view on
his recovery. The first thing apparent to his awakening
senses was himself, Theige of the Red Cloak, and Theige the
Wolf, bound hand and foot, sitting side by side, with osier
gads, or withes, round their necks, under the three ominous
branches of the Fairy Whitethorn. Immediately before them
stood a short, dark-browed man, who seemed calculating the
height of those three branches from the ground, and apparently having in his mind's eye a lively picture of three
men dangling in the intervening space. Around the tree, in
various attitudes, beside their horses, were the men of John
of the Bridle, who himself, with his lieutenant, Remy of the
Glen, stood a small distance outside the group, talking to
Alice O'Brien and Ellen Roche. There was a horrible light

in the eyes of both his comrades, which told Na Meerval too plainly what was to be their fate and his own.

"Where," exclaimed he, not yet able to collect his thoughts —"where is my skean gone to, that I had this minnit so rin in my hand? Ha! did I stab myself, that this blood is owin' down my back?"

"Go an' ask Remy o' the glen," answered Folling Dearg; that's the man that put the blood flowin' down your back, hen you should be protectin' yourself, instead o' raisin' your agger to the breast of a wake girl."

"Ha!" said Na Meerval, now fully awakened, "we're caught in our own thrap at last. My curse upon the two that had strong revinge in their hearts, an' their legs upon the free hills, an' couldn't escape from their worst inimies!"

"Were they free hills," exclaimed Cu Allee, with a wild volubility in his native tongue, "when they waited for us in the thickets, as the wild-cat waits for its prey; and when they sprang upon us, and bound us hand and foot, before we could find our dagger-hilts to defend ourselves? And are they free hills here, when we have the keen, torturing, and destroying gads about our necks, that will send us with strange, piercing pain, and mortal fear and anguish, into the other world?"

"Stop," answered Folling Dearg, with a sullen and ferocious look, "stop your pains and tormints: what is the torthure o' death to the tormints I feel at bein' bound this way, an' seein' him beyant there, talkin' to Alice O'Brien? Shane na Shrad," he continued, raising his voice, "I have but small time to live; but, if I had a thousant years, every day of id would be spent plannin' revenge, till I had sarved you as I sarved your lovin' frind, Moran O'Brien. My etarnal curse upon the fate—an' may the torrent dhry for ever in its bed—that tore you from my grasp!"

John of the Bridle made no reply; but, after saying a few words to the dark-faced man who was calculating the height of the branches, proceeded with Remy of the Glen and the two young maidens up the valley, and left the three Timothys to thir doom.

A few days after the death of the three Timothys, there was another merry dance on the green of Fannystown. But it was more of a novelty this time, for there was a bride and bridegroom to lead the measure; John of the Bridle—or Captain John, as he was at last entitled to be called—and Alice O'Brien having been joined heart and hand the same morning by the young priest who attended the cavalry force then occupying Castle na Doon.

Ellen Roche's sorrow was deep and true for her dead lover. But, as months wore on, time began to soften her grief; and she eventually became the bride of Remy of the Glen, John's lieutenant, whose timely blow rescued her from the dagger of the Man of Wonders.

Years upon years had passed away, until the grey fortifications of Kilcolman were level with the grass, and even the forests themselves were now dead upon the hills; but the ancient tree lived on in its solitude of Glenanar, regarded with a strange reverence by the peasantry, and still called by them " the Whitethorn of the three Timothys."

THE ROSE OF DRIMNAGH.

WHATEVER side we turn to, around the city of Dublin, we are sure to meet mementoes that carry our thoughts back to those turbulent days when sword and lance usually settled questions which are now adjudicated without disturbance, save an occasional battle of tongues, in our peaceful courts of law. Many of those ancient fortresses, which, like a crescent chain of watchful sentinels, towered beyond the city for the protection of the Pale, still remain, and raise their hoary heads over valley and river-shore, adown which, in bright array, plumed nobles, and steel-clad knights, and men-at-arms, rode gallantly forth to battle, where the weary creaght lowed, after the foray in which they had been driven from some far-off fastness of Imayle, Leix, or Ossory; and where the minstrel, half-Irish and half-Norman, once twanged his gittern as he went from castle to castle, relating, in rousing and voluble stanzas, the deeds of the knights of St. George. Among the most remarkable and interesting of these ancient structures is the Castle of Drimnagh, the subject of many a legendary tale. Could the bearded old warriors who once thronged its halls awake, they would witness many a wonderful change since the half-forgotten days when they lived and loved, revelled and fought, conquered or sustained defeat. Where the Asla, or mounted courier, once spurred forth upon his hasty errand, the lightning of heaven now speeds, by telegraphic wires, to the farthest corner of the land; through the craggy passes, and along the level plains, marked some centuries ago with scarcely a bridle-path, the mighty steam-horse thunders over its iron track with it ponderous load; and, instead of the small city which lay cooped up within its battlemented walls around the castle, a glittering panorama of streets and squares, docks, store-houses, towers, and splendid domes, now spreads outward to the capacious bay, where, in place of the crazy fleets of diminutive war-galleys and merchant-vessels, with their fantastic prows and carved mast-heads, the huge hull of the steam-propelled ship now rides at anchor beside the populous quays, or ploughs the blue waves beyond the hoary headlands of old Ben Hedar, like a miniature volcano, with its attendant cloud-volumes on the far horizon line.

Retaining still some of its ancient appurtenances, such as its moat, curtain-walls, etc., the Castle of Drimnagh presents one of the best specimens in the neighbourhood of Dublin of the ancient feudal stronghold. It stands beside the road leading from Crumlin to the village of Condalkin, and within a few short miles of the city. According to the most authentic accounts, it was founded in the time of King John, by a knight named De Bernival, who came to Ireland in the train of that prince, and received from him a grant of the surrounding lands. From this knight, the different families of Barnwell in Ireland claim their descent. His death occurred about the year 1221; and his descendants held possession of Drimnagh and Terenure till the time of James the First, when their possessions, after a tedious lawsuit, fell to Sir Adam Loftus. During the great insurrection of 1641, it was garrisoned for the king by the Duke of Ormond, and had the rare fortune of escaping the destruction that followed, after the arrival on these shores of Cromwell and his stern legions. It is still inhabited, and in good preservation, and will well repay the tourist who leaves the dust and toil and din of the city, and saunters out along the quiet country-roads, to pay it a visit. Should he linger there, and hold converse with the surrounding peasantry, he will hear many a story and romantic legend of days gone bye, the particulars of which will prove no unpleasing accession to his note-book. One of these we now proceed to relate, and hope it may prove as interesting to the reader as it did to ourselves, when we heard it told one quiet summer evening beneath the shadow of the ivy-wreathed battlements of Drimnagh.

During the reign of a certain English monarch, whose name we need not particularly mention, Sir Hugh de Barnwell ruled with a high and lordly hand in his feudal stronghold of Drimnagh. He was a stout and stern knight, whose life had been spent amid the commotions of the war that, year by year, raged between the Palesmen and the Irishry. Many a tough battle he had fought, and many a wound he had received, since he first donned the knightly spurs; and it will not be wondered at, therefore, when we mention that he looked upon the native races around with no small amount of hatred. Among those against whom his animosity burned most fiercely were the O'Byrnes, lords of Imayle, whose chief had once sacked his Castle of Drimnagh, and driven the herds pertaining to it over the southern mountain barrier, into Wicklow. The chief was still living at the time our story commences, and had two sons, the youngest of whom, named Sir John O'Byrne, was a knight of unwonted bravery. To his great personal beauty was added every accomplishment fitted for one of his high station; and when, at the head of his bold horsemen, he rode down the mountains, on a foray into the Pale, it would be hard to find, in the whole champaign over which he cast his eagle eye, a man of more splendid appearance and gallant bearing. Sir Hugh de Barnwell had one son, who was renowned throughout the Pale for his prowess, and for the ferocity with which he always fought against the neighbouring chief of Imayle. The following will explain his reasons for hating the O'Byrnes with such bitterness.   Living in his father's house, at the time, was his cousin, Eleanora de Barnwell, who, in consequence of her beauty, was called "The Rose of Drimnagh."   To this young lady Sir Edmond de Barnwell had been betrothed ; and matters went on smoothly and pleasantly enough for some time, .till, during a truce entered into between the Palesmen and the Wicklow clans, Eleanora met Sir John O'Byrne at a nobleman's house on a festival-day in Dublin.   Up to this, "The Rose of Drimnagh" knew little of her heart ; but she soon learned to love the young Wicklow chief, and, as a natural consequence, to look with coldness and indifference upon her cousin, who, at length coming to the knowledge of the affair, swore to be avenged upon his rival.   The truce was scarcely over, when he was up and at work ; and many a rifled hamlet and burning dwelling marked his track through the glens of Wicklow ; and many a desolate widow cursed his name and race as she sung the *keen* over the bodies of her slaughtered ones, who had fallen beneath the spears of Sir Edmond de Barnwell and his ruthless followers.

But at last a time came when a triumphant light shone in Sir Edmond's eyes ; for he thought upon the day, now near at hand, which was fixed upon for his marriage with the lovely Rose of Drimnagh.

"Once more," he said, "I will seek the mountains, to find him before the marriage revel.   By the soul of a knight, an' I lay my hands upon him, but he shall rue the hour !— yes, rue it ; for I swear to bring him in chains to look upon the bridal, and then to string him up, as I would one of his own mountain wolves, upon the gallows-tree, before the gate of Drimnagh."

It was nightfall as he spoke thus.   Little he knew that, at that same moment, Sir John O'Byrne was sitting quietly beneath the dark shadows of a tree outside the moat, look-ing up cautiously at the window of the little chamber in which Eleanora de Barnwell was sitting, weeping bitterly over the sad fate to which she knew but too well she would soon have to submit. As she sat thus, a low, soft sound, like the cooing of a dove, fell upon her ears. She listened intently a moment, then stepped softly over to the single window of the apartment, and, opening the casement, looked out. Again the sound stole up from under the dense foliage that shaded the outer edge of the moat. Eleanor leaned upon the sill, and peered down into the gloom; but nothing met her gaze, save the ghostly shadows of the trees upon the black belt of water beneath.

"It is his signal," she whispered to herself, as the sound was repeated once more. "Ah, me! I fear he will get himself into danger on account of these nightly visits. And yet I cannot, I cannot bid him stay away."

She muffled herself in a dark mantle, moved towards the door, opened it cautiously and listened, ere she ventured to steal down and meet her lover.

"I must and will warn him to-night to stay away," continued she, as, with a light and stealthy step, she descended the winding stair,—"ah! to stay away, and leave me to my misery. It is hard; but it must be done: otherwise he will assuredly be captured and slain."

After stealing down an infinite number of dark passages, corridors, and stairways, she at length emerged into the open air, and glided through a neglected postern, out beneath a spreading beech-tree that shaded the inner edge of the moat, opposite the spot whence the signal of her lover proceeded. Again she peered into the gloom at the other side, and saw there a tall, dark figure standing beneath a tree on the edge of the water. Well she knew the graceful outlines of that figure, and fondly her heart throbbed at the sound of the voice that now addressed her.

"Dearest," said the young mountain knight, in a low tone, "I thought thou wouldst never come. I have been standing like a statue against the trunk of this tree behind me for

... ast half-hour, watching for a light in thy window-pane. But it seems that darkness pleases thee better. Ah, Eleanora! I hope thou art not still indulging in those sorrowful forebodings."

"And wherefore not, John?" answered she sadly "What thoughts but gloomy ones can fill my mind, when I am ever thinking of the danger thou incurrest by coming here so often,—and thinking, too," she added, after a pause, "of the woful fate to which we are destined?"

"Think no more on't," said her lover, in a cheerful tone. "We have hope yet, Eleanora; for, mark me, thy marriage with Sir Edmond de Barnwell will never take place."

"Alas! there is no hope," resumed Eleanora. "Even to-day, my uncle, the Knight of Drimnagh, hath fixed the time for—to me—the woful bridal. And thou, John—let this be our last meeting, alas! in this world. Wert thou taken prisoner by my dark cousin, he hates thee so, that he would burn thee at a stake in the courtyard."

"Fear not for that, dearest," answered the young chief. "And this bridal that thou fearest. Listen, Eleanora. Before the hour comes, or, perchance, at the very hour when he is about to place the bridal-ring upon thy lily finger, the gay goshawk may swoop down, and bear thee away to his free mountains, amid their sunny glens and bosky woods, to love thee, darling, as no other mortal man could love thee."

"Ah me!" sighed poor Eleanora. "Would that it could be so! But I fear that we are fated to see each other for the last time to-night. I warn thee, John, to be wary henceforth; for I am well-watched. Hush! was that a foot-fall amid the grove yonder?" And she pointed to a clump of trees some distance to the right of where her lover stood.

"By my faith, but it may be so!" answered he; "and so thou hadst better return to thy chamber. In the meantime, I will wait here till I see the light in thy window once more, and until thou biddest me farewell from the casement."

The bold Knight of Imayle was not to be frightened away by the sound whatever might have caused it. Seating himself upon the side of the moat, in the shadow, and still looking fondly upward, he commenced, in a voice low, but distinct, a lay to his mistress, of which the following paraphrase may convey some idea :—

> "Oh! wilt thou come and be my bride?
>   Oh! wilt thou fly with me
> Where wild streams glide by mountain-side,
>   By glen and forest-tree?
> And thou'lt be lady of that land,
>   And like a queen shalt reign
> O'er shore and strand, and mountain grand,
>   And many a sunny plain!
>
> I've found a lone and lovely cave
>   Where gleams a little lake;
> Where the wild rills fling the silver wave,
>   And the birds sing in the brake:
> The lake gleams clear, the rills dance bright,
>   Down gorge and rocky pile;
> But the darkness of a starless night
>   Is in my soul the while.
>
> And nought can light it, save a glance,
>   A beam, from thy jet-black eye;
> And nought can break my heart's cold trance,
>   Save thy witching song or sigh.
> Then come! I've decked that cave for thee
>   With summer's fairest flowers;
> Away, away, o'er the hills with me,
>   To the forest glens and bowers!"

The moment the song had ceased, the fair form of the Rose of Drimnagh appeared at the casement overhead. She waved a fond farewell to her young mountain minstrel, and closed the window. He stood up, and, gazing once more at the casement that glimmered like a star amid the dark masses of masonry above, turned to depart, when he felt the heavy grasp of a steel-clad hand upon his shoulder.

"Stay!" exclaimed the intruder, in a deep, stern voice, whose tone the young Knight of Imayle knew but too well. "Thou hast a small account to settle, fair sir, ere thou leavest this spot. I am Sir Edmond de Barnwell."

" And I," answered the other, " am Sir John O'Byrne of Imayle : what seekest thou from me ? "

"That thou shalt soon know, skulking hill - cat!" answered De Barnwell, unbuckling his sword, unsheathing it, and throwing his belt and scabbard upon the ground. "There be a certain tide which men call blood, coursing beneath that breast-plate of thine. I seek to discover its fount with this ; " and he extended his weapon.

"There be a certain tide behind thee which thou art more likely to explore presently ! " retorted O'Byrne. " Ha, ha! beware the hill-cat's spring, De Barnwell!" and he gave a sudden bound that brought him inside the guard of his antagonist, whose waist he instantly encircled with his sinewy arms. There was an ineffectual attempt to pluck forth their daggers ; and then Sir Edmond de Barnwell was hurled from the stalwart arms of the brave Knight of Imayle, and sent plunging headlong into the black waters of the moat. Leaving his foe to scramble as best he could from his dangerous bath in the fosse, O'Byrne glided through the thickets, and sought his steed, which he had left in a lonely grove hard-bye, and was soon riding in headlong haste across the plain towards the stern mountain barrier that lay between. him and his native glens. And now De Barnwell, after extricating himself with great difficulty from the treacherous waters, stood, all dripping, upon the firm bank ; his burly frame quivering, not from the chill of his immersion, but from fury at his mishap. Pursuit of his late antagonist was, he knew, of little use now ; so, plucking up his sword which lay beside him, he raised the cold steel blade to his lips, kissed it, vowed a stern vow of vengeance against O'Byrne and his race, root and branch ; and then, striding down by the water's side, crossed. the drawbridge, and sought his chamber, where he sat, till long after midnight, brooding over various plans of merciless and bloody retribution.

The particulars of his subsequent cruel raid into the glens of Wicklow it is unnecessary to relate; and we shall now come to the day which his father had fixed upon for the marriage. It was early in the morning; and the fair Rose of Drimnagh, surrounded by her lovely maids, looked sadly upon the gorgeous white bridle-dress which lay on a table beside her, and which she was at last about to put on·

"Ah me!" she sighed mournfully, "that it hath come to this! In vain have I watched for him to appear in his accustomed place by the moat; but his promise is broken · and what could have broken it but death?" And the tears gathered into her eyes as she thought thus of her lover.

"Cheer thee, Eleanora!" said her cousin, a young and gay city dame. "I warrant thee that such a bridal as thine was never seen in Dublin : I only wish that I were in thy place."

"Alas, that thou art not!" returned Eleanora. "Something tells me that what thou sayest is but too true,—that such a bridle as mine was never seen." And with the help of her maids she now began to don her dress.

The marriage was to take place in the city; and Sir Edmond de Barnwell had summoned his kinsmen of the Pale, with all their fierce retainers, in order to strengthen his escort for the bridle-train, which at last, in splendid array, crossed the drawbridge of Drimnagh, and moved along the winding-road that led to the western gate of Dublin. This road was crossed by another, midway between the castle and the city, and within a wood which stretched down from the mountains to the shores of the Liffey. About half the bridal-train had passed the cross; and the remainder, with the bride and bridegroom before them, were moving gaily forward, when all at once the wild war-cry of the O'Byrnes resounded from the wood all around, and the next instant a large body of men, headed by the young Knight of Imayle, sprang from their concealment, and fell upon the escort, front, rear, and flank. It is needless to go minutely into details of the terrible fight that then took place at the Minstrel's Cross, as the spot was called. The escort were at first put to flight and pursued by the O'Byrnes; but, returning to the charge, the light kern of the mountains were borne down by their heavy horses, though they fought it out bravely to the last. The Knight of Imayle, after badly wounding the bridegroom, was shot through the heart by the old Lord of Drimnagh, as he attempted to seize the bridle of Eleanora's palfrey. This ended the fray. The body of the young knight was borne away by his followers, and buried in the lonely graveyard that lay amid the mountains. The bridal train, instead of proceeding to Dublin, returned to the Castle of Drimnagh, where Sir Edmond de Barnwell was laid upon a bed from which he never rose.

Three days after the fatal battle at the Minstrel's Cross, Eleanora disappeared from the Castle of Drimnagh. Search was made for her throughout the surrounding country, and even in the neighbouring city; but it was of no avail; she was nowhere to be found. At length a party of the O'Byrnes, who were driving a creaght of cattle across the mountains, halted beside the solitary churchyard to pay a visit to their young chief, and, upon the fresh sod that lay above his gallant breast, found the lifeless body of the ill-fated Rose of Drimnagh. They hollowed her a grave beside her lover; and there, in the words of the old ballad—

> " These loving hearts by fortune blighted,
> By sorrow tried full sore,
> In life apart, in death united,
> Sleep side by side for evermore."

THE FAIR MAID OF KILLARNEY.

A TALE OF ROSS CASTLE.

MONG the almost innumerable objects of interest that come under the observation of the tourist during his sojourn in Killarney and its neighbourhood, there is scarcely one whose examination will afford more pleasure than Ross Castle. Too many travellers there are, however, who either do not visit it at all, or, when they do so, pass it by with a glance, thoughtless and cursory. One, for instance, half-bewildered by the countless beauties of our Irish fairyland, will hurry away with a confused remembrance floating in his brain, of wild pass, silvery lake, rainbow-tinted island, and sunlit, sky-piercing mountain : another, equally alive to the natural beauties of that glorious scenery, but with an eye also for objects of legendary, antiquarian, and historical interest, will return to his home, the object of his tour only half-accomplished, for want of proper and reliable information regarding the various points of attraction he has met with during his visit. By far the greater number, however, with garrulous and flimsy guide-book in hand, flit about from Mucruss to the Devil's Punch Bowl, from the gap of Dunloe to the Castle of Ross, from island to island, and from mountain peak to lowland shore ; and carry away with them on their departure an incongruous medley of badly-told historical facts, hackneyed legends, and newly-invented nonsensical stories, all of which, they, of course, scatter liberally among their friends, both here and on the other side of the water, to the great discredit of that famed region which an erratic old gentleman of our acquaintance calls in his rapture, the " tourist's paradise." With the purpose of supplying to the tourist a few items of information of a less hackneyed character, we give, as a preliminary to our story, a short account of the spot in which its principal incidents were enacted.

Ross Castle consisted of a strong keep and other stout buildings, both of a domestic and military nature, surrounded by the usual bawn wall, with its breastworks and circular flanking towers at the corners. It is situated upon a peninsula on the eastern shore of the lower lake, and commands a view on every side of the wildest beauty and sublimity. Right before it, to the west, the lofty Reeks of Magillacuddy throw up their savage summits into the ever-varying sky; while to the south and east the horizon is broken by the steep, pyramidal crests of the Paps, and the Mangerton range of mountains. To the north, a number of abrupt and irregular summits shut in the view; and the traveller who looks from the time-worn battlements of the ancient stronghold will see around him a panorama of crag and wood, curving shore, fairy island, and glittering wave, far surpassing even the pictures of his wildest dreams of splendour and beauty.

The ross, or peninsula, on which the castle is built, was converted, if we may so speak, into an island, by means of a deep channel cut through the marshy neck by which it joined the mainland. This channel, or ditch, was filled by the waters of the lake, and formed the chief defence of the castle on the land side. It was crossed by a drawbridge, no traces of which now exist. Regarding the precise date of the foundation of the castle, or the name of its founder, history is silent. It was probably built by some warlike chief of the O'Donoghoe sept, in the midst of whose immense territory it stands. From the style of its masonry, and other characteristics, it does not seem older than the latter part of the fourteenth century. About that date, and in several parts of Ireland before it, the Irish chieftains began to adopt some of the manners of their powerful Norman neighbours; and upon the sites of their wooden *cahirs* or fortresses, built strong castles of stone, in which they stood many a gallant siege; and from which, at the head of their followers, they often rode forth in wild array, to protect their borders against those mail-clad invaders whose trade was war, and whose perpetual law was the strong hand, and the might of battle-axe and sword.

During the vengeful wars that then raged throughout the length and breadth of Ireland, Ross Castle frequently changed owners. From the O'Donoghoe More, by one of whose ancestors it seems to have been erected, it passed into the hands of Mac Carthy More, by whom it was transferred, in the year 1588, to Sir Valentine Browne, ancestor of the present House of Kenmare. Passing over its various reverses during the latter Desmond wars, we will proceed at once to the most remarkable period of its history, namely, its surrender to the Parliamentarian forces under Lieut-Gen. Edmond Ludlow, in the year 1652.

After the dismemberment of the Confederation of Kilkenny, several of the generals who had fought under its banners, still held out stoutly for their native land, against the Puritans. Among these was Donogh Mac Carthy, Lord of Muskerry, chief commander, in Munster, of the Catholic forces. After his defeat at the battle of Knockniclashy, in the county of Cork, he led fifteen hundred men across the mountains, and threw himself into Ross Castle, the last stronghold of importance at that time in possession of the Irish. Thither he was followed by Gen. Ludlow, into whose possession the castle fell after a short siege. The manner in which the castle yielded to the Parliamentarian general, will be best understood by a perusal of our story.

At the commencement of the great insurrection of 1641,

Ross Castle and the surrounding territory belonged to Sir Valentine Brown. Sir Valentine was at that time a minor, under the guardianship of his uncle, who was afterwards slain in one of the battles fought during that destructive and protracted war. The warden of the castle, towards the termination of the war, in 1652, was a distant relation of Sir Valentine, named Richard Browne, a captain in the confederate army. Capt. Richard Browne had an only child, a daughter, named Mabel, who lived with him in the castle. Mabel, at the time, was just verging into womanhood, and was a lovely girl; so beautiful, indeed, that she was called by the surrounding people, of every degree, " The Fair Maid of Killarney." It will not be at all wondered at, therefore, that the young officers who commanded under her father in the garrison should have been smitten by her beauty. Foremost among those who paid her homage was a young man named Raymond Villiers, a lieutenant of musketeers, and a descendent of a stout English settler who had come into that country about a century before.

Raymond Villiers was the possessor of a small but good estate, lying upon the shore of the Main, a river that empties its waters into Dingle Bay. The Veteran warden of the castle was well acquainted with the circumstances of the young lieutenant of musketeers, and looked favourably upon his attentions to Mabel; but the latter persisted in receiving the homage of her suitor with no small amount of coldness, the reason of which will be understood presently. Thus matters stood between the young pair, until the day of the battle of Knockniclashy, in which, as was seen above, the forces of Lord Muskerry were defeated by the troops of the Parliament, under Ludlow.

The sun of that disastrous day was setting beyond the wild mountains of Dingle, as Capt. Browne was standing upon the battlements of the castle, taking a survey of the warders beneath, as they walked to and fro, in their monotonous avocation, behind the breastworks of the massive bawn wall beneath. Lake and island and giant hill lay bathed in a flood of golden glory around him. The blue smoke from the tall chimneys of the castle curled up in airy columns through the calm summer sky, and the slumbering quietness of the whole scene seemed to exert its soothing influence upon the mind of the grey-haired warden; for, after taking a quick survey of the sentinels below, he sat himself upon a small brass falconet, or cannon, that commanded the drawbridge, and began musing silently for some moments.

" By my faith," said he at last, " but I wish this war was ended, and my daughter married to young Raymond Villiers! I could then sit down quietly for the remainder of my days, and turn my thoughts to another world, which, alas! I have little time to think of in this time of foraying and slaying. Rory," continued he aloud to a wiry little sunburnt boy who usually attended him on his rounds, "go and tell Mistress Mabel that I am here, and that I want to speak to her for a few moments."

Rory disappeared in an instant down the winding stairway; and, after a little time, Mabel Browne made her appearance on the flat space on the summit of the castle, and sat down beside her father.

"Mabel," said the latter, looking affectionately upon his daughter, "I have been thinking that this wooing of Raymond Villiers has gone far enough, and that you ought to give him a favourable answer."

Now, it must be premised that Mabel, only child as she was, took some liberties on that account, and usually contrived to have her own way in the end, no matter how her father threatened and stormed. Whenever she saw his brows darkening, she usually succeeded, by dint of alternate crying and coaxing, in brightening them again; but, on the present occasion, she knew, by the fixed look of determination in her father's face, that he was at last bent on carrying his point.

" I cannot tell, father," she answered, " why it is that

you are so eager to get rid of me in these troublous times. As for myself, I would rather stay with you to the end of my days; and you know also very well that you cannot do without me. Think," continued she, with a smile of mingled reproach and fondness upon her lovely face, " only think of the time, two years ago, when you sent me to spend the summer with my aunt in Tralee, how you fretted and neglected yourself during my absence, and how, at last, you had to send for me, and could not bear me away ever since."

"No matter," answered her father. " Times are changing now, Mabel. I am growing old and infirm, and there is no knowing the day that I may fall in battle, or die of this cough that is now continually troubling me;" and he pointed to his stout chest, which, if the truth must be told, showed but little signs the ravages of the complaint to which he alluded. "If it should come to that," continued he, " whom will you have to protect you during the troubles?" And he looked into his daughter's face knowingly, as if he defied her to get over the stumbling-block he had propounded.

"Oh! as for that, father," answered Mabel, "I trust in God there is but little fear of it, seeing that you are the strongest man in the garrison. Remember that I saw you myself last week, leaping your horse over the Wolf's Hollow, a feat that does not show very much weakness or infirmity ;" and she gave the gratified old soldier another of her fond, roguish smiles.

" I tell you, Mabel," rejoined he, trying to look sour in spite of himself, " no matter how affairs go with me, it has come to this, that I have set my heart upon your marrying Raymond Villiers; and marry him you shall, for he is in every way worthy of you."

" I am sure he is," returned Mabel, " and deserving of a far better wife than I would make him ; but"—

"But what?" interrupted her father. "That's the way you are always putting me off. I hope, Mabel," he continued. in a yet more energetic tone, " that you are not still thinking of that wild spendthrift, Donogh of Glenmourne."

A bright blush overspread the features of Mabel Browne at the sound of that name. She looked upon her father reproachfully, her eyes all the while gradually filling with tears.

"If I am, father," she said mournfully, " I cannot help it now and then. You know there was once a time when you did not forbid me to do so. However," she continued with a sigh, " I will try to forget him since you wish it ; but I cannot, I cannot give my heart to Raymond Villiers, be- cause"—

" Because he is not worthy of it, I suppose you will say," said her father somewhat bitterly. " But know, Mabel, that Donogh Mac Carthy of Glenmourne is now landless, and has nought save his sword to depend on ; and, by our lady, but that's but a weak prop to depend on in these dangerous times!"

"I know it," returned Mabel, her eyes brightening as she thought of her absent lover. " I know that he was robbed of his estate by Cromwell; but that is no reason why I should play him false."

"I knew that was the answer you would make," said her father; "but, notwithstanding, you must wed, and that soon, with Raymond Villiers. Ha! what is that I see? Look, Mabel, look! I trust in God, whoever it is, that he brings us good news!" And he pointed towards a slope at the eastern side of the castle, down which a horseman was riding towards them in furious haste.

"There must have been a battle fought!" exclaimed Mabel, looking eagerly upon the approaching courier, as he still rode on, his helmet and trappings glittering in the red beams of the setting sun. " See! he is facing directly for the drawbridge. My God! it is he, it is he!" And again the red blood mounted to her cheeks, and the tears sparkled in her eyes, as she became conscious of exhibiting such unusual emotion before her father.

"Who is it?" asked the latter eagerly. "Your eyes are sharper than mine, Mabel; and I do not know him yet."

"It is Donogh of Glenmourne!" exclaimed Mabel, scarcely able to restrain herself from darting down the stair to welcome the coming of the young horseman.

"I know him now," said her father. "Look at his horse all covered with foam and mire! Look at his plume shorn off, and the sad plight he is in! He is the bearer of bad news." And with that the old veteran left his seat upon the cannon, and hurried down the stair, followed by his daughter.

With a hasty step, he strode to the drawbridge, which, by his orders, was immediately let down to give ingress to Donogh of Glenmourne, who, in a few moments afterwards, rode inwards, and dismounted in the courtyard; where he was soon surrounded by an eager throng, all burning to hear the news with which he was sent thither. The tidings he brought were sorrowful enough; and shouts of anger, and execrations, deep and fierce, were muttered by his hearers, as he told them how, that morning, Lord Muskerry was vanquished in the battle of Knockniclashy. After giving this disagreeable bit of information with a soldier's brevity, he followed the warden of the castle to a private room in order to deliver some further instructions with which he had been charged by his general after the battle.

Donogh of Glenmourne was as good a specimen of the young Irish officer of the time as could well be seen. He was about twenty-five years of age, strikingly handsome, tall of stature, and had that bold, frank bearing that so well became his degree, which was that of a captain of cavalry. To the owner of a pair of bright eyes that watched him eagerly from a little window overhead, he now appeared doubly interesting as he walked forth once more in his battle-soiled armour, and joined a little knot of officers who were conversing in the court-yard. For a few moments only Mabel regarded him, and then hastened down to her father to hear the tidings.

"I fear, Mabel," said her father, "that you will have but a sorry time of it henceforth. Lord Muskerry is now marching with the remnant of his forces across the mountains, and will be here early to-morrow. He will, of course, be followed by Gen. Ludlow; so I think you had better get ready and go to your aunt at once; for we are about to stand a siege."

"I cannot leave you, father," said Mabel; "so do not send me away. Whatever happens, I would rather stay with you; and, besides, you know that I am safer here than I should be in Tralee."

"Perhaps it may be so," returned her father; "but we will think it over. In the meantime, I must go and give directions to have the castle ready for Lord Muskerry and the somewhat large force he is bringing with him." And he walked out, and speedily called the garrison to arms. The noise of preparation soon rang from end to end of the huge fortress. At last, night settled down upon hill and lake and tower; and all became still, save the tread of the wary sentinels as they paced to and fro along the ramparts.

The ramparts of Ross Castle were now crowded with men; and all was busy preparation for the expected siege. Some of the broken Irish regiments were also encamped in the surrounding woods; so that Gen. Ludlow, when he invested the castle with an army of about six thousand men, had a game to play as difficult as it was dangerous.

Matters were in that condition, when one evening Mabel stole up to the battlements of the castle in order to obtain a view of the hostile camp. Plainly enough it lay, almost beneath her, towards the east; the arms of its occupants all

flashing and glittering in the sun, and the painted banners
flaunting proudly in the eveuing breeze. As she stood gazing with curious eye upon that martial scene, she heard a
light step behind her, and, turning round, beheld Raymond
Villiers approaching from the stairway, with a somewhat
troubled look upon his dark and handsome features. He
sat himself upon the battlement beside her, and for some
time neither spoke. His troubled and somewhat diffident
manner might be easily accounted for by the fact that he
had then and there determined to try his last chance of getting a favourable answer from Mabel. The single warden
who watched from the summit of the castle was standing
upon a small pinnet, or tower, at the opposite side, and could
not hear their conversation, which at last Raymond Villiers
wound up his courage to begin.

"I have sought you, Mabel," he said, "for many reasons.
This siege must soon be ended; for I am sure the fortress
cannot hold out against yonder splendid and brave army,
and then there will be many changes. You will see, then,
why I am anxious to understand your sentiments towards
me."

"I pray you," returned Mabel, with a cold smile, "to
explain to me, Master Villiers, why the castle cannot hold
out. Surely, Lord Muskerry is strong enough to hold his
own here at least, where he has a deep lake, a goodly
trench, and a brave castle crowded with men to back him."

"That may be," said Villiers. "But there seems to be
some curse upon our cause. Everything goes badly with
us; and why should this castle hold out when stronger ones
have fallen?"

"This is language that ill befits a soldier," answered
Mabel, smiling contemptuously. "You, Master Villiers,
were wont to boast loudly enough whilst the enemy was far
off. Now that he is near us, it seems strange that you cannot keep your heart up, like a brave man, in the emergency.

Do not expose yourself too much, I pray you," she added, with another smile of contempt. "Keep in shelter of that battlement beside you, else yonder gun that the enemy seems arranging in the battery on the height may pick you off ere the siege is well begun."

Nothing is so maddening to a lover as a word or smile of contempt from the woman he loves. The temper of Raymond Villiers was hot and violent; and Mabel's tone and look enraged him beyond measure, though he strove to hide his anger.

"I did not come to discuss military tactics," he said, with a forced smile. "I am here, Mabel, to decide my fate with regard to you; and thus I ask you, for the last time, will you become my wife when this siege is over?"

"Nay," returned Mabel, "it would be indelicate of me to consent so hastily, seeing that the siege, as you say, is to come to so speedy a termination. So," she continued in the same ironical tone, "I cannot grant your request."

"I have dallied long enough," muttered Villiers, a frown, in spite of himself, darkening his features. "This is to be my final answer, then," added he, turning to Mabel: "I am to understand, that in spite of my devotion, and in spite of all your father's commands, you will not consent to be my wife?"

"No," returned Mabel, firmly; "for my father will never force me to it."

"You will not, then?"

"No. And now, Raymond Villiers, let us put an end to this for ever. You know I cannot be your wife, and you know also the reason of it."

"Yes," exclaimed Villiers, bitterly, "I know it. *He* is here, and you love him. But we will see to it—by the breath of my body, but we will see to it!" And he stood up, and, bowing coldly to Mabel, took his way down the stairway, with a black and revengeful frown upon his swarthy brows,

A week had now passed away. It was midnight. Beneath the black gloom that shrouded lake and castle and giant mountain, a tall figure, muffled in a long military cloak, glided along the rampart towards a sentinel who stood beside the western turret, facing the water. The sentinel turned, and demanded the watchword for the night. It was given; and the tall figure moved down to the water's edge, and, stepping cautiously into one of the three small boats that were moored beneath the shadow of the tower, took the oars, and shoved it silently out into the lake. By and bye another muffled figure, evading the observation of the sentinel in the darkness, stole silently beneath the rampart, and stepping into one of the remaining boats, put it off in a similar manner. The first boat glided noiselessly across the lake, and, at last, landed its occupant upon the shore, above which was situated the camp of the Parliamentarians. The second, also, followed stealthily in its wake; but, stopping some distance from the shore, turned back again, after a short time, towards the castle. As it glided in beneath the shadow of the western tower, the figure which it bore left it, and soon gained the court-yard unobserved. It then glided up a stairway of the castle; and, entering a little chamber, the long cloak that muffled it was cast upon the floor, and the lovely face of the Fair Maid of Killarney was revealed in the light of a small taper that was burning upon a table near the fireplace.

"Whoever he is," she said, as she sat herself beside the table, "he is a traitor. But I will wait and watch; and assuredly I will find him, or my name is not Mabel Browne."

Meanwhile let us follow Raymond Villiers; for he it was that had gone upon his dark midnight mission across the lake. After narrowly escaping being shot by the advanced sentinel of the enemy, he contrived to make his purpose known, and was soon conducted into the presence of Gen. Ludlow.

"What dost thou want?" said the stern Puritan general.

in a surly tone at being awaked from his first slumbers. "Why didst thou not come in the light of the day with thine errand, whatever it is?"

"For the best reason in the world, general," answered Villiers. "If any of my own people saw me, my life would not be worth a silver crown. I come from the fortress yonder."

"Ha!" exclaimed Ludlow, "I begin to understand thee now. What of the castle? and hast thou any method by which we can take it speedily?"

"You will never take it by your present tactics," answered Villiers; "for the garrison is well manned, and they have abundance of provisions, besides the natural strength of the place. I am a lieutenant of musketeers. If I succeed in gaining you a passage across the drawbridge, or point out another method by which you can take the castle, will you give me the same rank in your army?"

"Gladly, gladly!" answered Ludlow, who knew but too well the strength of the garrison. "And now, in case thou canst not betray the drawbridge to us,—obtain passage over it for us, I mean,—what is thine other method?"

"There is a prophecy regarding Ross Castle," answered Villiers, "which the majority of those who now defend the castle believe in with their hearts and souls; and, when they see this accomplished, I will stake my life they will yield the castle to you on the easiest terms. It is this,—that Ross Castle can never be taken till the enemy sail in a fleet of ships upon the lake. Can you not accomplish the prophecy?"

"I think so," answered the Puritan general, after a long pause, during which he sat thinking intently. "Ho, there!" continued he to the grim orderly, who stood guard at the door of his tent: "summon hither Scout-master-general Jones, and say that I want to consult with him on a most important matter."

In a short time, the scout-master-general made his ap-

pearance ; and there followed a long consultation, at the
end of which Raymond Villiers took his departure, and succeeded in reaching his quarters in Ross Castle unobserved.
The result of Ludlow's consultation was, that, in case Villiers failed in otherwise betraying the castle, Scout-master-
general Jones undertook to procure and transport from
Kinsale to Castlemain Bay, and thence overland to the
Parliamentarian camp, the materials, ready made, of a fleet
of heavy gunboats, with which they could attack the castle
from the lake.

Two days passed away, during which Villers found that
there was but small chance of betraying the drawbridge of
the castle to the enemy. He therefore finally resolved to
leave the place, and go over as secretly as he could to the
hostile camp. It was thus, that, about midnight, he contrived to procure a boat as before, and make his way across
the lake. This time, however, Mabel Browne, who con-
stantly watched his motions, and who now sat concealed
beneath the dark shade of the wall, knew his features as he
glided past, and followed him, as she did the other night,
over the water. As he stepped upon the land, an unlucky
splash of Mabel's oar caught his ear. He stood, and peering outward through the darkness that overhung the water,
caught sight of the boat and the figure that sat therein,
which he, of course, thought was that of a man. A fierce
frown of vengeance contracted his dark brow ; and, drawing a long pistol from his belt, he fired at the indistinct
figure. The next moment a wild shriek of agony and terror
rang over the dark lake ; and Mabel Browne, with her arm
broken between the elbow and shoulder, dropped like a
wounded bird into the bottom of the boat. Fortunately, a
smart breeze was blowing at the time from the eastward,
and floated the boat towards the opposite shore of the lake,
else the poor wounded maid of Ross would have fallen into
the ruthless hands of the Parliamentarian soldiers.

The report of the pistol, and the wild shriek of Mabel, were followed by loud confusion in castle and hostile camp. Each side thought that the pistol shot was a signal for an attack of some kind. Men hurried to and fro by rampart and trench. The cannon on both sides opened fire for a short interval; but at length all settled down quietly again, and the night passed away. Little did they know that night, in the Castle of Ross, of the terrible agony their warden's daughter endured beside the solitary shore of the lake, to which the boat was driven by the breeze.

The dawn was faintly tinging the eastern sky, when the Fair Maid of Ross awoke from one of the long swoons into which she had fallen since she had received the treacherous shot of Raymond Villiers. There was now light enough, but she had scarcely sense left to look around her. Her arm was lying helplessly by her side; her dress and the bottom of the boat were all stained with blood; and, with a faint scream of anguish, she dropped back again into her former position in the boat.

When she next awoke to consciousness, it was with a cooling and somewhat pleasant sensation. She opened her eyes; and the first object they fell upon was the welcome and pitying face of Donogh of Glenmourne. He was standing over her in the little boat, washing the blood from her neck and arm, and sprinkling the cool water gently over her face. All was soon explained. When she told him, as well as her weakness would permit her, of the treachery of Raymond Villiers, and how it was from his murderous shot she had received her wound, Donogh swore a stern oath, that, ere many days should elapse, he would avenge the deed surely and suddenly upon the head of his perjured rival.

Meanwhile the siege went on. The Parliamentarian general pushed his approaches nearer and nearer to the castle; and the cannon and small arms on both sides rattled away most industriously every day from morning until night.

About ten or a dozen days after the occurrence of the fore-
going events, two horsemen might have been seen riding in
wild haste over the mountains, and approaching the north-
western shore of the lake. It was Donogh of Glenmourne
and one of the dragoons belonging to his troop. Leaving his
horse to the care of his orderly, Donogh descended into a
secret nook by the water's side, and was soon rowing a little
boat he had taken therefrom, across the lake to the Castle of
Ross. The news he brought was, that Scout-master-general
Jones, with a skilful engineer named Chudleigh, had just
landed in Castlemain Bay, with a vast quantity of timber
ready hewn for large boats, and was now on his way across
the country to the camp, escorted by a strong convoy of the
Parliamentarians, horse and foot. After giving this news,
he again crossed the lake, and soon joined his troop, with
which he hovered upon the track of the approaching convoy.
As the latter passed through a narrow defile, he fell upon it,
sword in hand, with his men, and had a sharp skirmish. He
was, however, finally repulsed, but not till he had the satisfaction of knocking Raymond Villiers on the head with his
own hand, and thus ending the new career that gentleman of
an easy conscience intended running, under favour of the
Parliament.

The convoy arrived safely at Ludlow's camp; and the
boats, under the superintendence of Chudleigh of Kinsale,
were soon put together and fit to be launched. One fine
morning, when the garrison of Ross awoke, they were not a
little astonished to see a fleet of ships, or, in other words, large
gunboats, floating upon the lake, with cannon ready pointed
at their bows, and colours flying jauntily overhead. All
cried, with one voice, that the fatal prophecy was fulfilled,
and that the castle could hold out no longer. Lord Muskerry,
seeing the despondent spirit that pervaded his little army,
demanded a parley with his enemy. The end of it was that,
after a long debate, a capitulation was drawn up; and Lord

Muskerry yielded the Castle of Ross, on very honourable terms, however, to the Parliamentarian general. This put an end to that terrible war which devastated the country for so many years.

Immediately afterwards, Donogh MacCarthy rode over the mountains with a score of his bold horsemen, and dispossessed the Puritan undertaker who held his House of Glenmourne. The Puritan, perhaps seeing plenty of estates, far larger and richer, going almost for nothing around him, prudently made no noise about the the affair; and thus our young captain of cavalry entered once more into possession of his home, in which he and his descendants were confirmed after the restoration. Some months after the yielding of the castle, Donogh of Glenmourne was made doubly happy by his marriage with the Fair Maid of Killarney; and with the light-hearted pair, it is said that the stout old warden, Capt Richard Browne, lived afterwards, for the rest of his days a life of jovial ease and contentment.